BROKEN SILENCE

BADGE OF HONOR SERIES

LYNN SHANNON

BROKEN SILENCE

Copyright © 2026 by Lynn Shannon Balabanos

Published by Creative Thoughts, LLC

All rights reserved.

No part of this book may be reproduced in any form or by any electronic or mechanical means, including information storage and retrieval systems, without written permission from the author, except for the use of brief quotations in a book review.

This book is a work of fiction. Names, characters, businesses, organizations, places, events and incidents either are the product of the author's imagination or are used factitiously. Any resemblance to actual persons, living or dead, events, or locales is entirely coincidental.

Cover design by Maria Spada.

Scripture appearing in this novel in whole or in part from THE HOLY BIBLE, NEW INTERNATIONAL VERSION®, NIV® Copyright © 1973, 1978, 1984, 2011 by Biblica, Inc.™ Used by permission. All rights reserved worldwide.

The Lord is close to the brokenhearted and saves those
who are crushed in spirit.

Psalm 34:18

ONE

An icy wind whispered through the abandoned train depot, rattling the broken chain-link fence like an ominous warning.

Special Agent Peyton Hughes shivered as she exited her pickup. Dark shadows clung to the rusted railcars and the broken husk of the service station. Her vehicle was the only one in the parking lot. Where was Lilia? Had she not arrived yet? It seemed unlikely, given the frantic phone call she'd made to Peyton.

You have to come. Please. There's no one else I can trust, and it's life or death.

It'd been nearly three years since Peyton had last seen or spoken to her younger cousin, but nothing in their rocky relationship would prevent her from showing up when Lilia was clearly in trouble.

A clang reverberated from somewhere deep inside the train depot. Peyton peered into the darkness, trying desperately to make out distinct shapes among the shadows. "Lilia?"

Her voice carried across the parking lot, but silence was the only answer. Goosebumps skittered over Peyton's skin. She didn't like this. Not one bit. Pulling her cell phone from her pocket, she dialed Lilia's number. Her cousin didn't answer. Just like the last five times Peyton tried to reach her.

The nerves plaguing her during the two-hour drive from Dallas grew in intensity. Lilia had been thin on details, promising to explain everything in person, but the thread of fear thrumming through her voice had been all too real. Was she hiding somewhere in the depot? Her phone could've run out of battery. Lilia had never been violent—not even while high—but she hung out with a cast of unsavory characters. At least she used to. Peyton didn't know what Lilia was like these days. Still, it wasn't hard to imagine her cousin had gotten ensnared in a dangerous situation and was in over her head.

A career in law enforcement—first as a state trooper and now as a Special Agent with the Texas Department of Public Safety's Criminal Investigation Division—had taught Peyton to trust her instincts. It wasn't smart to search the train depot for Lilia without backup. Knoxville, Texas wasn't a hotbed of criminal activity, but like all small towns, it had its problems. And the depot attracted all kinds, from drug users looking to get high to homeless individuals seeking shelter against the harsh winter nights. Tonight, in particular, was biting. The temperatures were predicted to reach freezing.

Peyton bit her lip. She needed to call for help. A state trooper would be the easiest option, but there was no guarantee one would be available or nearby. The next best option was reaching out to the local police department, but calling dispatch meant explaining the situation to a stranger, waiting for them to relay the information, then hoping a patrol officer wasn't already tied up with another call. That could take twenty minutes. Maybe more. Time, Peyton sensed, Lilia didn't have.

Which left only one option. There was only one person who would understand the situation immediately, who knew Lilia's history, who could be here in minutes, and was trained for these kinds of situations.

Dawson Graham. A detective with the Knoxville Police Department.

Her ex-husband.

Peyton's chest tightened and her fingers gripped the cell phone. Another icy wind rattled the broken chain-link fence. For a moment, she considered bailing. Hopping into her pickup truck and hauling herself back home to her quiet apartment, far away from the ghosts of her past and the pain of her mistakes. But the fear vibrating in Lilia's voice held her in place.

Her cousin had begged. Peyton had made a lot of mistakes in her life, but she'd never ignore a cry for help.

She pressed her lips together and punched in the numbers she knew by heart on her cell. The first ring had barely trilled on the line before a deep voice tinged with just the hint of a Texas accent filled her ear.

"Graham."

An ache she hadn't expected, or hadn't had time to anticipate, swept through her. Her mouth opened, but it took a second before she could speak. "Dawson."

Silence followed. She sensed his shock. Or maybe it was disbelief. They hadn't seen or spoken to each other since their final divorce proceeding five years ago. A divorce she'd initiated, and he'd never wanted.

"I'm sure... I know this isn't..." The words tangled in her throat, and Peyton momentarily lost her voice and her courage. Then she drew in a sharp breath and reminded herself that this was a professional call, not a personal one. "I need your help, Dawson. It's a matter of life and death. At least... that's what Lilia said. She called me earlier this evening, desperate and terrified, and asked me to meet her at the abandoned train depot. I'm here now, but there's no sign of her. It's possible she's hiding out, afraid of someone. I need to search the area, but don't want to go in alone."

"Stay put. I'll be there in five minutes."

No hesitation. No questions. The vise gripping her chest loosened. "Thank you, Dawson."

His only reply was to hang up. Peyton tucked her cell phone back into her pocket before adjusting the zipper on her jacket. It was bitterly cold. Her breath fogged in front of her. Weak moonlight peeked through the clouds overhead, and she searched the shadows again. A piece of cardboard fluttered from the broken window of the service station, and the air was scented with the acrid smell of old grease and decay. It would be far warmer to wait for Dawson in her vehicle, but she kept hoping Lilia was watching from somewhere nearby and would materialize from the shadows.

Peyton leaned against the cold metal of her pickup. Five minutes. It seemed like an eternity. Long enough to manifest fresh anxiety about seeing Dawson again, not to mention dozens of troubling scenarios that would've caused Lilia to call after three years of radio silence. What had her cousin gotten herself into?

She scanned the depot again. Nothing moved. Silence pressed in from all sides, heavy and expectant.

Peyton's thumb drifted absently across her left ring finger. The skin was smooth where her wedding band used to sit. That ache in her chest spread. She'd thought of Dawson often, especially in the last few years. Considered calling him to apologize for the way things ended, but in the end, she didn't. It seemed unfair after what she'd done.

They'd been so happy. High school sweethearts who beat the odds and stayed together through college. They married, started their careers, and then a few years later, Peyton fell pregnant. Both of them had desperately wanted children, and it felt like finally everything in her life was falling into place.

Then her grandmother, Nana Grace, died suddenly. Peyton had been devastated to lose the woman who raised her, and she clung to her unborn son like a lifeline.

At six months, preeclampsia struck without warning.

Samuel Thomas Graham was stillborn.

And something inside Peyton broke. She lost her sense of self. Her dreams. Even her faith. She felt as if

God was punishing her. Church, which had once been a haven, now made her angry. Dawson's steadfastness, his kindness, and his grace were salt on her wounds. He went back to work, his friends, his family. And she'd hated him for it—hated that he seemed capable of surviving a loss that was destroying her.

She'd ended their marriage at the kitchen table.

I can't do this anymore. I look at you, Dawson, and all I see is everything we lost.

He'd fought her on it, but Peyton was beyond listening. She'd been hollow and so lost in grief she couldn't see straight.

It'd taken years—and a nearly fatal car accident—before she finally sought help. She found her faith again, and therapy helped her process the mountain of unresolved trauma and grief she'd been carting around. Peyton was proud of the woman she'd become. It'd taken a long time to get here. But there was also regret. Dawson had deserved better. And now? After five years of silence, she was selfishly calling him for help. She prayed he would forgive her for it.

Peyton exhaled, her breath a pale ghost in the moonlight. She shoved the memories back behind the wall where they belonged and focused on the depot. Five minutes had to be nearly up. Where was—

A scream pierced the night.

High-pitched. Terrified. Female.

Lilia.

Peyton's hand flew immediately to the weapon holstered at her waist even as her feet moved toward the break in the chain-link fence. Heart pounding, eyes scanning, she slipped into the train depot. Her scarf snagged on a jagged edge of the cut fence, pulling the fabric from her neck. She barely felt the frigid wind slipping down the back of her jacket. Urgency fueled her steps as she maneuvered past train tracks toward the west end of the depot and the sound of the scream. Her combat boots were silent against the gravel. The scent of grease and oil turned her stomach.

Another blood-curdling cry echoed through the night air. Further away this time. Closer to the woods surrounding the far edge of the property. Common sense urged Peyton to stop, to call Dawson and inform him of her movements, but fear for her cousin kept her in motion. Adrenaline coursed through her veins. She pressed herself against the wall of a railcar. The icy metal bit through her jacket, seeping into her skin, all the way down to her bones. She shuddered.

Movement out of the corner of her eye sent her pulse racing. Peyton raised her weapon, catching a flash of dirty clothes and a bearded face before the homeless man slipped back into the darkness of a rusted shipping container. She exhaled sharply. Loosening the grip on her weapon, Peyton purposefully took three deep breaths to counteract the narrowing of her vision. Then she peeked around the corner. Faint moonlight glimmered on the trees surrounding the far edge of the property.

No sign of Lilia.

A faint whimper reached her ears. Peyton held her breath and strained to listen. It sounded like it was coming from inside the railcar. Was Lilia inside? Hurt and in pain? The entrance to the car was just around the corner, but the moonlight trickling in through the clouds would expose Peyton to anyone watching. She searched the woods and the surrounding area. Nothing stirred. But the pinprick sensation of danger nearby gave her pause. Was the homeless man in the container watching her from the shadows? Or was there someone else?

A shadow drifted across the moon, casting the entire area into darkness. Peyton knew she wouldn't get a second opportunity. She pivoted around the corner and hurried toward the entrance, pausing at the set of steep stairs leading into the railcar. Impenetrable darkness yawned. Another faint whimper reached Peyton's ears. The sound was strange, but she couldn't place why.

"Lilia?"

The harsh whisper went unanswered. Someone was in there though. Peyton couldn't turn back now, nor could she spend time second-guessing her decisions. Gritting her teeth, she grasped the frigid metal and hauled herself up the first step.

The blow came from behind. Hard. Sudden. Pain exploded across Peyton's skull as her knees crumpled, bouncing off the unyielding metal stairs before the gravel rushed up to meet her. Instinct sent her rolling. She rammed into a concrete barrier, the impact strong enough to rattle her teeth, but she had the presence of mind to raise her gun.

A dark figure lunged. She squeezed the trigger, but

her shot went wide as a massive fist connected with her wrist.

Her weapon clattered across the gravel.

Within seconds, he was on her. She fought back, but whoever the attacker was, he had skills and sheer strength on his side. Darkness hid his face. His body pinned her. Rocks dug into the bare skin at the nape of her neck as he pushed one gloved hand against her throat. Stars danced across her vision as the last of the air in her lungs became trapped.

Then the familiar sensation of a gun barrel pressed against her temple.

TWO

Detective Dawson Graham white-knuckled his steering wheel as he turned onto the rutted road leading to the train depot parking lot. He'd driven most of the way through town with his lights and sirens on, but had killed both about a mile back. If Lilia was hiding out, as Peyton suspected, she might not react well to unexpected police presence.

Of course, Peyton was a cop too. But that was different. She was family.

His headlights swept across a familiar blue truck. Peyton's. The old Ford still sported a dent on the rear bumper and a Sam Houston State University bumper sticker. Seeing it sent a swirl of emotions through Dawson. He remembered the day she'd bought it. On her eighteenth birthday. She'd saved every penny from working at the local coffee shop, counting and recounting her money until she finally had enough for a down payment. The smile on her face when the salesman handed her the keys had been breathtaking. Pure joy. Unfiltered hope for the future.

He also remembered watching that same truck pull out of the courthouse parking lot five years ago, taillights disappearing into traffic. The day their divorce was finalized. It was so vivid, he could recall the feel of the drizzle on his face and the hollowed-out sensation in his chest.

Dawson shoved the memories aside and killed his engine. Icy air smacked him in the face. Discarded paper and leaves blew across the potholed asphalt, and an itch between his shoulder blades had him assessing the abandoned service station with suspicion. He wouldn't be surprised to discover several people were holed up inside, seeking shelter from the cold. Although he'd arrived without his lights and sirens, in his experience, druggies and other petty criminals could smell a cop from miles away.

Most of them would steer clear. A few might like a chance to even a score.

Dawson had no intention of letting that happen. To him, or to Peyton. It'd been reckless of her to agree to meet her cousin here, especially in the dead of night, and more so given Lilia's penchant for trouble. But Peyton had always had a soft spot for Lilia. The two women had been raised together by their grandmother, Nana Grace, and were more like sisters than cousins. Now that Nana Grace was gone, Lilia was one of the last family members Peyton had left.

Keeping one eye on the service station, Dawson approached Peyton's vehicle. His senses were so focused on potential threats that it took him several paces to realize she wasn't in her truck. His gaze swept the shadows in the parking lot. No sign of her.

The chain-link fence rattled, drawing his attention to the opening. Something flapped against the metal. Dawson closed the distance and reached for the item caught on the fence. A scarf. It was too dark to tell the color. Blue? Maybe red? He lifted the wool to his nose and drew in a breath. Jasmine. This was Peyton's scarf.

His anxiety ratcheted up. She'd gone in alone.

Peyton might be a touch reckless, but she was no fool. If she hadn't waited for him, there'd been a good reason. Something was very wrong. Dawson unholstered his handgun and then pulled his cell phone from his pocket. He dialed dispatch and requested backup. He'd barely gotten the words out when a gunshot split the night air.

Terror for Peyton sent his pulse skyrocketing. He shoved his phone into his pocket and moved through the gap in the fence, weapon up, shoulders low. Training overrode panic. Clear the corners. Use cover and keep to the shadows. Broken glass and bits of rock crunched under his cowboy boots as he moved farther inside. Adrenaline threatened to narrow his vision. He slowed his breathing to counteract it.

Please, God. Please don't let me be too late.

Peyton had been part of his life since he was sixteen years old. She'd been his first love, his wife, the mother of the son they'd lost. There was grief, disappointment, and sadness—a canyon of hurt between them that still kept him up at night. That sometimes made him angry. He'd stood in a church and vowed before God to love her for better or worse, and meant it. He'd *kept* his word. And she'd walked away. From them. From him.

Dawson didn't think Peyton could break his heart any more than she already had, but if he found her dead...

He'd never be the same.

The sound of a struggle reached his ears. Dawson rounded the corner of a shipping container and saw them. Two figures locked in combat near the base of a railcar. Even in the dim moonlight, he recognized Peyton's smaller frame. She was fighting—twisting, striking—but the man had brute strength and clear combat skills on his side. He threw Peyton against a rail-car. She bounced off it like a rag doll, slipping to the ground.

"Police! Freeze!" Dawson's voice cut through the night.

Metal sparked inches from Dawson's head, the metallic clang echoing in his ears. He dove behind the shipping container as another bullet embedded itself where he'd just been. Heart pounding, he lifted his head to catch the flash of a muzzle near a concrete barrier next to the woods. A second assailant. Dawson raised his gun and returned fire. He swung his gaze back to the first attacker and Peyton.

The man was gone. Crashing sounds in the nearby brush indicated he'd taken off into the woods.

Dawson rose to a crouch, his gun held at the ready. He waited for one breath. Two. The gunman hiding behind the concrete barrier remained silent. Had he run away too, like his comrade? Chances were the answer was yes, but it would be foolish to jump to conclusions. Keeping to the shadows, he circled around the back of the container before taking cover beside the railcar. Peyton wasn't visible.

"Peyton?" His voice was low, barely above a whisper.

"I'm here." A shadow shifted from underneath the railcar. "Are they gone?"

"I think so." Dawson waited a few more seconds before closing the distance between him and Peyton. Sirens wailed in the distance, uncoiling some of the tension in his muscles. Backup was close. He crouched next to Peyton's side. The scent of her jasmine perfume tickled his senses and threatened to toss him into the past. Shadows kept her features hidden. Still, relief cascaded through him. She was alive. Breathing.

Dawson removed his cell phone from his pocket. He flipped on his flashlight, covering it with his hand to dim the glow. "How badly are you injured?"

"I'm fine. I almost had him too."

Her tone was layered with enough irritation that it made his lips quirk. But any amusement faded as his flashlight caught the soft lines of her face. Blood darkened the strands of her chestnut-colored waves, and welts in the shape of fingers marred the creamy skin at her neck. Bits of grit and dust from the gravel coated her clothes. Her jeans were torn on the left knee.

If hearing her voice on the phone had been a gut-punch, seeing her was a full-body blow. Dawson's heart stuttered. Emotions he couldn't put words to tumbled through him, but overriding all of them was the instant desire to comfort her. To draw her into his arms and carry her to safety. He battled against it, but wasn't able to stop his fingers from gently grasping her chin and tilting her head to get a better look at the cut. "You've got a nasty head wound."

"He knocked me off the stairs, and I dropped my weapon." Peyton lifted her handgun. "I retrieved it after he threw me against the railcar. While you were exchanging gunfire with the other guy, I got off a shot of my own. It didn't seem to slow him down, but he stumbled. I might've winged him." She started to get up.

Dawson pushed to his feet and extended a hand. Peyton waved off his help, choosing to use the railcar instead. The rejection was slight, but it burned all the same. "Why didn't you wait for me?"

The question came out rougher than he'd intended, and a spark of annoyance flared in her hazel eyes. "I heard a woman scream. Lilia."

And of course she'd run in without backup, because that was Peyton. Always moving toward the people who needed her, regardless of the cost to herself. It was one of the things he'd loved most about her. In this case, it'd nearly gotten her killed. But discussing the recklessness of her actions would only put her on the defensive, so instead, he focused on the case. "Did you see her?"

"No, I heard whimpering from inside the train car." She took a step toward the stairs and nearly crumpled to the ground.

Dawson reacted instinctively, his arm wrapping

around her slender waist. Even in the dim light, her complexion was pale. Freckles sprinkled on her nose, normally faded in the wintertime, stood out in stark relief. "You need to sit down."

"I'm fine." She sucked in a deep breath and pushed away from him before straightening her shoulders. "Just a bit of dizziness. That's all."

She wasn't fine. Not even close. But the set of her jaw told him pushing would only make her dig in harder. Some things hadn't changed. Peyton had always been complicated and infuriatingly stubborn. Incredibly brave too.

A sudden wail emanated from inside the railcar. It cut off, and then whimpering followed. Dawson hurried to the metal staircase, Peyton on his heels, moving far faster than he would've thought possible given her head injury. He shone his flashlight into the darkness. Nothing but rusted metal. He'd have to go inside.

Gun raised and flashlight up, he navigated the steep stairs. He swept the light across the small space. In the rear was a pile of discarded boxes. The whimpers were coming from there. They sounded human. His boots shuffled against the dusty floor, and motes danced in the beam. Peyton's hand touched his back. Like him, she had her gun raised. Her breathing was shallow, but her expression was determined.

"Knoxville Police Department, make yourself known." Dawson's voice reverberated off the metal. A sharp cry followed.

And suddenly, he knew.

His steps quickened. Dawson tossed aside the cardboard.

A baby—only a few weeks old—lay strapped in a carrier, wearing a pink snowsuit. Her tiny fist was pressed against her mouth, her dark eyes wide under the brim of a knitted cap. A small backpack sat next to her.

Behind him, Peyton inhaled. Shock seemed to render her motionless.

Then the baby looked at Dawson and wailed.

THREE

Grace Elizabeth Morrison.

Peyton stared at the name on the birth certificate that'd been tucked underneath the cover of the baby carrier. The scents of antiseptic and stale coffee soured her stomach. Or maybe it was the painkillers the emergency room doctor had given her. The lump on her scalp throbbed even through the painkillers, promising a migraine later. A cart rattled as someone pushed it past the room.

"You didn't know Lilia had a baby?"

Peyton looked up from the birth certificate to Dawson. He stood at the foot of the bed, his expression a careful mask of indifference. Built like an ox, with broad shoulders that strained the fabric of his jacket, he cut an intimidating figure. The badge hooked to his belt, along with his holstered weapon and quiet confidence, radiated authority. Dark curls—trimmed short and neat—drew attention to his strong jaw, shadowed now with stubble.

The past five years had added a few crow's feet to the corners of his rich brown eyes, but they only made him more attractive.

Her heart skipped a beat, an unconscious reaction that cut through her shock. Peyton forced herself to focus, turning her attention to the baby nestled in a clear bassinet. Like Peyton, little Grace had been examined by the emergency room doctor. He'd declared the one-month-old in perfect health.

Peyton, on the other hand, had a concussion. They were waiting for the results of her MRI to determine if she could leave tonight, or if she'd have to stay in the hospital for observation.

"No, I didn't know Lilia had a baby." Regret and guilt pinched her, threatening to unmoor the careful hold she kept on her emotions. "We had a falling out three years ago. Tonight was the first time I've seen or heard from Lilia since."

"What was the falling out about?" Detective Liam Miller asked from his perch on a chair near the window. Like Dawson, his expression was flat and nonjudgmental. Peyton vaguely remembered Liam from high school. He'd been a senior when she was a freshman. The intervening years had been kind. Muscular and clean-shaven, he'd ditched the thick glasses for contacts, revealing a set of stunning baby blues.

But Peyton saw past his even tone and good looks. She recognized the way he surreptitiously studied her. Liam hadn't decided if she could be trusted, and she wondered how much Dawson had told his colleague about their past. Neither of them had lived in Knoxville when they got divorced. Both had been working in Dallas back then.

Dawson would never speak badly of her, but Peyton was smart enough to realize Liam's loyalty would be to her ex-husband. Rightfully so.

"Money. Lilia showed up at my house high, looking for a place to stay and cash. We argued." She winced, remembering the harsh words her cousin had hurled at her. Peyton hadn't been in a good place herself, still mired in grief and working herself to the bone. Her temper had gotten the best of her. The fight had devolved quickly. "She refused to check into rehab, and I threw her out. She disappeared after that. I tried to contact her last year, hoping to make amends, but her cell number was no longer working."

"So you were surprised when she called asking for help?"

"Yes and no. This is the longest Lilia and I have gone without talking, but we've had periods of estrangement before. Mostly when she was using. It used to be, when she needed help, she'd call our grandmother. After Nana Grace died, Lilia turned to me." She smoothed out a wrinkle in the sheet. "I guess... I figured one day she'd pop back into my life."

"And Lilia didn't tell you why she wanted to meet you at the train depot?" Liam asked.

"No. She only said she was in trouble and needed my help. Lilia promised to explain everything in person." Worry plagued her. Knoxville police officers and state troopers were currently combing the train depot, searching for any sign of her cousin. Peyton fiddled with the edge of her sheet. "Maybe I should've insisted on more information, especially given her prior history with addiction, but she sounded so scared... and I knew she had to be desperate if she was calling me after all this time."

Liam asked a few more questions, but Peyton couldn't provide any helpful information. The man who attacked her at the train depot had been wearing a ski mask. She only had a vague description to give him—roughly six feet tall and fit. "There was a homeless man nearby though. Caucasian, with a thick beard, wearing sweatpants and a tan wool jacket. He disappeared into the shipping container when he saw me. Maybe he spotted Lilia earlier. Or witnessed the attack on her. I'm certain the scream I heard was my cousin."

"The responding officers will interview everyone they find at the train depot, but I'll make sure they keep an eye out for the man you've described." Liam shifted his weight and pulled his cell phone from his pocket. He glanced at the screen. "Sorry. I have to take this. Be right back."

The door swung softly shut behind him. An awkward silence followed. Peyton felt small and vulnerable in the hospital bed, but didn't quite have the wherewithal to stand. She also couldn't bring herself to look at Dawson. Instead, she focused on baby Grace's birth certificate. Lilia's name was typed out in all caps on the official document under mother, but the space for father was left blank. "There's no father listed. That's weird, right?"

Dawson shrugged. "Maybe he didn't want to be involved."

"Probably so. Lilia never had good taste in men." The letters on the birth certificate swam as sudden tears filled her eyes, catching Peyton off-guard. She was scared to death for her cousin. Despite their years of estrangement, she loved Lilia deeply. Had longed for the return of the sisterly bond they'd shared as children.

Would they have a chance to reconcile? The sound of Lilia's screams kept replaying in her head, and Peyton didn't need a decade of law enforcement training to know her cousin was in danger. Mortal danger.

A tear escaped, trailing down her cheek before she could hide it.

Dawson's footsteps were soft against the tile as he approached. In the next second, she was enveloped in his embrace. The scent of his aftershave—cedar and citrus—filled her senses. Peyton's head found the curve of his shoulder instantly, muscle memory taking over. Comforting. Warm. Anchoring. She sank into his touch as memories rose unbidden in her mind. Long walks in the park, dancing under the shade of an old oak tree to soft country music, tender kisses full of promises and love.

"We'll find her, Peyton." His voice was low, rumbling through his chest and vibrating gently against her ear. "Everything is going to be okay."

"I hope so." She pulled away to reach for some tissues, wiping her face, before crumpling them in her hand. "Thank you, Dawson. For coming tonight. It means a lot, especially given how things ended between us." She forced herself to meet his gaze and drew in a breath. "I owe you a long-overdue apology. I was angry after Samuel died, and..." Shame heated her cheeks. "I couldn't see a way forward. I lost my faith in God. It took me a long time to find my way back."

His jaw tightened. "Neither of us handled it well. I made my own mistakes." Dawson shifted from the bed to a chair. His expression was neutral, but she heard the warning note buried in his voice. "Why don't we leave the past in the past? There are bigger issues to deal with at the moment."

He didn't want to talk about this. Typical. He'd never handled tough conversations well, and this time, she couldn't blame him. What good would rehashing the past do? It couldn't be changed. Dawson was right to focus their attention on Lilia's disappearance.

A knock on the door preceded the emergency room doctor. His white coat flapped as he approached her bedside. "Good news, Ms. Hughes. Your MRI shows only a mild concussion. We're going to send you home, but I want you to get plenty of rest and hydrate. If you experience any dizziness, severe headache, vomiting, vision changes, or confusion, I want you to come right back." He continued rapid-fire, with a list of instructions while checking her pupil reaction. "The nurse will be in shortly with the discharge paperwork."

"Thank you, Doctor."

He left the room, closing the door hard enough that it

jolted baby Grace. She gave a hearty cry. Peyton struggled to detangle herself from the bedsheets. Her muscles screamed in protest.

"I've got her." Dawson rose and effortlessly slipped a hand underneath Grace's head before gently lifting her into his arms. The baby immediately quieted. Dawson's head dipped, his focus on the little girl, and in an instant, Peyton was transported back in time.

Her, in a hospital bed. Dawson standing nearby, his face etched in anguish as he held their son.

Samuel. Sweet Samuel.

A grief so painful it was physical swept through Peyton. All at once, she felt hot and cold. Her fingers found the necklace at her throat—Nana Grace's cross— and held on. She forced a shallow breath. Then another one. The heartache subsided. Not completely. It was there, always. There were times, like now, when something would trigger a forceful reaction, but more often than not, it was a dull ache. But it didn't consume her anymore. She'd learned to let it pass through without pulling her under.

Still, her hands trembled, and the room felt too small. She pushed back the sheets and swung her legs over the side of the bed.

Dawson looked up, concern flickering in his eyes. "Are you okay?"

"Yeah." She managed a small smile. "Just give me a minute. I'll be right back."

She didn't wait for his response. The bathroom was only a few steps away, but her legs felt unsteady—

whether from the concussion or the weight of her grief, she couldn't tell. She closed the door behind her and leaned against the sink, staring at her reflection. Her complexion was pale, dried blood still crusted in her hair.

You're stronger than you know, baby girl. The Lord didn't give you a spirit of fear, but of power, and love, and a sound mind. Remember that.

Nana Grace had said those words before they entered the church for her mother's funeral. Peyton clung to them now. God was with her, and He would see her through.

She splashed water on her face and then washed as much of the blood out of her hair as possible, while being careful of the tender knot on her scalp. Feeling centered and more like herself, she stepped back into the hospital room.

Dawson was sitting in the chair next to the bed, still holding Grace. He glanced up, that concern still riding his brow. "Feeling better?"

She nodded. Peyton braced for a pang of grief, but this time, it didn't come. She drifted closer. The baby had fallen back to sleep, long lashes resting on chubby cheeks. Her tiny rosebud mouth worked softly, as if she were dreaming of a bottle. Peyton could see the echo of Lilia in the curve of the baby's forehead and the line of her jaw. She also shared their chestnut-colored waves. "She's beautiful." Peyton paused. "Lilia named her for our grandmother. Grace Elizabeth."

Dawson nodded. "Nana Grace would be proud."

"She would be."

Their gazes met, and an understanding passed between them. One that could only come from having known each other since they were sixteen years old. Dawson had spent hours at her house with Nana Grace. She'd been like a grandmother to him too. He'd loved her nearly as much as Peyton and Lilia had.

Dawson tilted his head toward the baby. "Would you like to hold her?"

"Yes, but I'm not steady enough yet." Her muscles felt weak, and she didn't want to drop Grace. Peyton smiled down at the little girl. "And she's so peaceful in your arms. I don't want to disturb her."

He was quiet for a beat. "Peyton, there's something you should know. We found something else tucked in the baby carrier along with the birth certificate."

Her stomach tightened. "What?"

A knock on the door interrupted their conversation. Peyton gave permission for the person to enter, expecting the nurse with her discharge paperwork. Instead, an older man wearing a Knoxville Police Department uniform came in. His salt-and-pepper hair was trimmed short, and his expression was no-nonsense.

He stepped forward. "Ms. Hughes, I'm Sam Garcia, Chief of Police."

Her muscles stiffened. The chief of police hadn't shown up in her hospital room to deliver good news.

She braced for what would come next.

FOUR

The weight of the baby in his arms added extra significance to a case already layered with complications. Dawson had never been fond of Lilia. As a teenager, he'd found her shallow and petty and unruly. During the years he was married to Peyton, he grew to have more sympathy for her wayward cousin, but Lilia's addiction and manipulative ways made her destructive. She hurt Peyton. Repeatedly. So much so, it'd strained even Dawson's patient and forgiving nature.

But for all Lilia's faults, she was Peyton's family.

Chief Garcia's arrival sent a cascade of dread through Dawson. His boss wouldn't be here unless the news were bad. And Peyton—who'd already survived more loss than most people endured in a lifetime—would have to, once again, weather more pain.

"Have you found Lilia?" Peyton's voice came out strong, but there was a slight tremble in her fingers before she pressed her hands to her sides. Her posture was rigid, shoulders back. She was close enough that Dawson could take her hand, but he resisted.

She wasn't his wife anymore. He needed to remember that.

Chief Garcia glanced at Dawson before settling back on Peyton. "No, ma'am. We haven't found Lilia yet."

Peyton's exhale of relief was audible, and matched Dawson's own. She crossed her arms. "But you found something."

"Signs of a struggle and blood near the back fence, close to the woods. Our search-and-rescue dog picked up a trail, but it ended abruptly, as if Ms. Morrison was taken away in a vehicle. A search of the area yielded little evidence, although my officers will try again in the morning." Chief Garcia rested his hands on his duty belt. Despite the late hour, his uniform was crisply pressed, but shadows darkened the skin under his eyes and the lines bracketing his mouth were more pronounced. It made him seem far older and wearier than his years. "Does your cousin have any connection to the Iron Serpents?"

A crease formed between Peyton's brow. "The Iron Serpents? I'm not familiar."

"They're a local biker gang." Dawson rose and gently placed the still-sleeping Grace into the bassinet. "On the surface, they're a social club, but we've linked them to drugs, prostitution, and weapons." The Knoxville PD had been trying to shut them down for years to no avail. It was like playing whack-a-mole. For every member they arrested, two more were recruited to replace him.

"And you think Lilia was involved with them?" Peyton directed the question to Chief Garcia.

"We recovered a bandana with the Iron Serpents logo in the woods, near the site of your attack. It's a lead we're following."

Peyton sighed and then sat back on the edge of the bed. "I'm not sure who Lilia has been involved with. We haven't spoken for the last three years. Given her troubled past, I wouldn't rule out the possibility though." She glanced at the baby, concern darkening her hazel eyes. "Whatever happened, Lilia was scared. And judging from the way she hid Grace, she was desperate to protect her daughter. So desperate, in fact, she called me. I have to believe she was trying to do the right thing."

Dawson looked down at the sleeping infant in the bassinet. Grace's tiny chest rose and fell with each peaceful breath, completely unaware of the danger that had surrounded her hours ago. Peyton was right. Whatever else Lilia had done wrong in her life, tonight she'd been trying to save her daughter.

"My aunt may be able to tell you more about who Lilia was in contact with lately." Peyton addressed Chief Garcia. "And if she had any connection to the Iron Serpents."

"That's Lilia's mother?" the chief asked.

Peyton nodded. "Sandra Morrison. She used to live off Budde Road in a trailer, although I haven't seen or spoken to her since my grandmother died six years ago, so I don't know if that's still the case."

Dawson wasn't surprised Peyton had cut all contact

with her aunt. Sandra was a long-time alcoholic, and a mean one to boot. She and Peyton had never been close, and Lilia's continued contact with her destructive mother had been a sore spot between the cousins.

"We'll find her." The chief scribbled a note on a pad of paper he'd unearthed from his front pocket. "What about Lilia's father? Or any other close relatives that might provide more information?"

"Lilia's dad was never in the picture, and there are no other close relatives. It's her mom. And me."

"Friends?"

Peyton shook her head. "I have no idea, Chief. Sorry. I can't even tell you where Lilia's been living since I last saw her."

"That's all right. You've given us a place to start." The chief offered an understanding smile. "I understand the doctors are releasing you and little Grace. I've already spoken to the caseworker and sent her the guardianship paperwork. She's agreed to allow Grace to stay with you for the evening, but you should touch base with her tomorrow morning—"

"Me?" Peyton blinked in shock. "I'm sorry. You want *me* to keep Grace?"

Chief Garcia's brow crinkled in confusion. "Forgive me, I just assumed, given the guardianship paperwork, that you wanted Grace to stay with you." His gaze swung toward Dawson. "Was I misinformed?"

"Actually, sir, I haven't explained." Dawson turned toward Peyton. Her wavy locks framed her face, falling around her shoulders, brushing against the deepening bruise on her right cheek. The hospital staff had found her a pair of scrubs to wear, but they were two sizes too big for her slender frame. "This is what I started to discuss with you before the chief came in. Along with the birth certificate, we found guardianship paperwork tucked in the carrier. Lilia named you as Grace's guardian."

Her eyes widened. "What?"

He crossed the room and picked up a sheaf of papers tucked in a folder before handing them to Peyton. She flipped through the legal documents. Her hands trembled as she scanned the pages, and Dawson watched her face drain of color. When she looked up at him, there was something raw and panicked in her expression before she quickly shuttered it. "Is this why she called me? To take Grace?"

"It's possible. Until we find her, we won't know for sure. But these guardianship papers make things a lot easier for everyone because they allow you to take Grace now. The caseworker will alert the court in the morning, and there may be a hearing, but there's no reason to believe the judge won't allow Grace to stay in your care." He paused, letting that sink in, and then continued softly, "Lilia called you because she believed you'd protect her child. This baby needs you."

She looked up at him. Steely determination replaced the shock. "You think Grace is in danger."

He shrugged. "We can't know for sure, but those guys already had Lilia, and they still came back. For what? We've looked through the backpack Lilia hid with Grace.

There's nothing in it besides baby supplies." Dawson rubbed the back of his neck. "The probability that Grace is in danger is minimal, but it's something we can't rule out yet."

"Dawson's right," Chief Garcia intervened. "But Ms. Hughes, taking Grace is your decision. If you don't want the responsibility, I'll keep her location secret and do everything in my power to protect her. Would you like a few minutes to think about it?"

She straightened her shoulders. "No. I'll take her."

"Are you sure?"

"Yes. Hopefully, Lilia will be found within the next few hours, and this nightmare will be over." Her fingers brushed against her temple, near her head wound, as if it was aching. "I'll need transportation back to the train depot to collect my vehicle. And I guess I'll stay in a hotel nearby. The Limestone Inn near the highway should do."

"You can't drive with a concussion," Dawson interjected. His voice softened as he took in her exhaustion and the blood still matted in her hair. She'd been through the wringer tonight. "I'll take you to the hotel tonight and arrange for some officers to drop off your vehicle there after the crime scene is processed."

Peyton offered him a smile of gratitude. "Okay."

Chief Garcia tilted his head toward the door. "Dawson, may I have a moment, please?"

His tone was polite, but there was no question that the chief had given an order. Dawson dutifully followed his boss to a small alcove. Voices from the nurses' station filtered down the hallway, and the brightness of the fluorescent lights hurt his eyes. He braced himself for the discussion.

When Chief Garcia faced him, there was no judgment in his gaze, only concern. "I'm not one to insert myself into the personal lives of my subordinates, but it's no secret this case is personal to you. You don't need to drive Peyton and Grace to the hotel. I can have Liam do it."

Logically, it might be smart to wash his hands of this here and now. Let Liam take Peyton and Grace to the hotel. His colleague would ensure they got there safely, and Peyton was an armed law enforcement officer, more than capable of handling herself.

And yet... Dawson couldn't bring himself to take the out. He was in this, and had been from the moment Peyton called. No matter their history and the hurt between them, he would never abandon her.

"I appreciate the offer, sir, but it's unnecessary." Dawson straightened his shoulders. "She called me for help, and I want to see this through."

The chief studied him for a long moment and then nodded. "If that changes, you'll let me know."

"Of course, sir."

As his boss walked away, Dawson took a moment to breathe. Doubt niggled as he second-guessed his decision all over again. It'd take a long time to heal the wounds Peyton had carved in his heart, and already, he could feel her wriggling past his defenses. The history between them was complicated, as were most things in adulthood, and some inner wisdom—maybe faith, maybe just age—

urged him toward grace. Peyton had been thrust into a difficult situation, and she was facing it alone.

He couldn't let her do that. Not when she reached out for his help. So he'd stay. Protect her. Solve this case, and then say goodbye.

For good this time.

FIVE

Darkness pressed against the truck as the bright lights of the hospital faded in the distance. Peyton felt some of the tension in her body loosen as the familiar sights of Knoxville flowed past her window. Charming red-brick buildings flanked by wide sidewalks and large oaks. Dawson eased to a stop at a red light. The cheerful awning of Roasted Beans fluttered in the light breeze, and across the street the last customers were trailing out of Ruby's BBQ. A smile lifted her lips as Ruby herself came into view, calling out to a woman who'd forgotten her cell phone. They exchanged a few words together and a laugh, and then Ruby lifted a hand in farewell before slipping back inside to lock the door.

Home. She'd missed it.

"Are you sure you don't want to stop by Ruby's for something to eat?" Dawson asked from the front seat of his SUV. His gaze met hers in the rearview mirror. "She won't mind keeping the kitchen open a bit longer."

"No. I can grab something light at the store. I'm not that hungry." Peyton glanced at little Grace nestled in her car seat. She'd gobbled down a bottle at the hospital and was now in a milk coma. Her chubby cheeks were tinged with healthy color and dark strands of wavy curls peeked out from underneath the brim of her knitted cap. She was precious.

Lilia's child. And, at the moment, Peyton's responsibility. Love and terror mingled together into a ball she couldn't detangle. The last few hours had been utterly surreal.

The light switched to green and Dawson pulled away from the intersection. The buildings of Knoxville faded into the distance as they headed for the highway. Grace stirred in her car seat, screwing up her face, and then a sound erupted from underneath the blanket that sent Peyton's eyebrows into her hairline.

"What is happening back there?" Dawson's mouth quirked in a teasing smile. "You okay, Peyton?"

A laugh bubbled up. "That was not me!" More toots came from Grace. "Good gracious, she's worse than a grown man!" Peyton dissolved into giggles. Dawson's accompanying laugh was effortless and contagious.

Then Grace opened her big brown eyes and cried. The mirth faded as a slight panic hit Peyton. She didn't have any experience with babies. None. While pregnant with Samuel, she and Dawson had taken parenting classes at a local church, but lessons about diaper changes and proper ways to hold an infant were a distant memory. "What's wrong with her?"

"She probably needs a fresh diaper." Dawson pulled into the parking lot of a big box store. He found a spot close to the entrance and hopped out before opening Peyton's door. His easy smile put her at ease as he extended a hand to help her out of the vehicle.

Peyton hesitated and then slipped her fingers into his. Muscles, injured during the fight at the train depot, hurt with every move. Although she smothered the wince, Dawson, ever perceptive, placed his other hand on her elbow to steady her as she stepped to the ground. His touch, along with his nearness, sent her heart skittering. She did her best to ignore the reaction.

Dawson grabbed the backpack from the floorboard and lifted Grace from her car seat. His nose wrinkled. "Woof! Yep, she needs a diaper change, all right."

They hurried inside and found a family bathroom. Dawson lowered the baby changing station and laid Grace on it. "We'll need wipes and another diaper." He deftly slid the soft cotton pants off Grace and winced. "And another change of clothes."

Peyton opened the backpack and found neatly organized supplies, including a plastic Ziplock bag meant for the soiled clothing. She watched in fascination as Dawson quickly changed Grace's diaper and dressed her, all the while speaking to the baby in soft tones and sweet words. The baby seemed equally enchanted by him, her dark eyes latched to his face. She gurgled and waved her hands.

Dawson glanced up, catching Peyton staring. "What?"

"I..." She blinked. "You're so good with her."

"I've got an army of nieces and nephews now." He lifted Grace from the changing table, wrapping her in a fresh blanket. "Claire and her husband had twins last year. Those minions are running the show. Then Marcus and Jessica welcomed their new baby last month. Izzy and Oliver are thrilled to have a little sister."

Joy swelled as Peyton followed Dawson out of the restroom. Izzy had been an infant the last time she saw her, and Dawson's sister Claire hadn't been married. "Twins? That's wonderful. And Marcus must be over the moon."

"He is. Though he's also exhausted." Dawson's entire face lit up as he talked about his family. His eyes twinkled with mischievousness. "You should see my little brother trying to wrangle three kids under the age of five. I think Mom's secretly thrilled to see our family troublemaker get his due."

Peyton laughed. She pushed the shopping cart while Dawson carried Grace. He helped her pick the right diaper size and navigate the formula aisle. He suggested they purchase the same brands Lilia had in the backpack. Peyton picked out several sets of clothes for herself, along with other essentials, since she hadn't brought anything with her to Knoxville. As they exited the store and drove to the hotel, their conversation flowed easily. Dawson amused her with stories about his family. Peyton was genuinely happy for them. The Grahams deserved every blessing.

Despite his cheerful demeanor, Dawson never

stopped watching for trouble. It was a reminder of every-thing they'd been through tonight. Peyton didn't believe the attackers would risk a second assault, but with evidence suggesting her cousin had been embroiled with a biker gang, it was smart to be cautious.

Relief flooded over her when they reached the Lime-stone Inn. The modest two-story hotel wouldn't win any awards for luxury, but it was fairly priced and exception-ally clean. Checking in was a breeze, and after a short ride up the elevator, Peyton opened the door to her corner room. Designed like a small apartment, it had a tiny living room and adjoining kitchenette. The clerk had assured her there was a crib already set up, and sure enough, it sat in the corner of the bedroom.

Dawson laid the bags from the store on the kitchen table. "Would you like me to keep an eye on Grace while you clean up?"

It was a generous offer. Peyton's hair was still matted with blood, and a hot shower would go a long way to soothing her aching muscles. But the hours in Dawson's presence had unlocked a longing she'd spent years desperately trying to forget. Even now, she wanted to step forward and hug him, feel his strong arms surrounding her. With him, she'd always felt safe.

These feelings were dangerous. Dawson had been friendly, but there was a guardedness to his interactions with her. If Peyton wasn't careful, she'd end up leaving town with a broken heart. Besides, he'd already done so much for her. It wasn't fair to take advantage of his good nature and generosity.

Peyton hugged her arms around herself. The oversized scrubs were scratchy against her skin. "No, thanks. Grace will sleep for another half hour or so. That'll give me enough time to shower before she needs to eat." The baby was nestled in her car seat and hadn't stirred through the entire trek through the hotel.

Dawson shifted his feet. "Okay." He hesitated and then cleared his throat. "Sure you'll be okay here by yourself? I can sleep on the couch—"

"No." The word came out forcefully. She softened it with a smile. "You've gone above and beyond, Dawson, but I'll be fine." Peyton patted the backpack, which carried her holster and weapon. "I've got my gun, and if there's a hint of trouble, I promise to call the police."

His mouth curved up. "I wasn't talking about attackers. I was thinking more about Grace. With your concussion and other injuries, it might be easier to have a second pair of hands helping care for the baby."

"Oh." She glanced at Grace, and a moment of hesitation and worry creased her brow. Could she take care of Grace all by herself? She'd never spent longer than ten minutes alone with a baby before, and after the poopy diaper incident, it was clear she was out of her depth. But nothing would be solved by relying on Dawson's help. She was responsible for Grace, and sometimes diving in the deep end was the only way to learn.

Peyton focused back on Dawson. "I'll muddle through. How hard can it be to keep one tiny human alive for a few hours?" She winked. "If Marcus can do it, then I can too."

He chuckled. It was warm and deep, and attraction flickered through her. She'd always loved his laugh.

Definitely time to get him out of here. Peyton strolled to the door and opened it. "Thanks again, Dawson."

"Sure thing." He followed her lead, but then hesitated on the threshold. His hand cupped her bicep. "You'll call if you need anything."

"Yes, yes." She rolled her eyes to hide the way her pulse raced at his touch. The warmth of his skin sank through the thin fabric of her scrubs. She felt it all the way to her toes. "Now get out before I have to literally kick you to the curb."

He smiled, as she hoped he would, and squeezed her arm. "Night."

She closed the door behind him and leaned against it. The impact of his touch lingered. Regret and longing and heartache tumbled through her, the storm of emotions too furious to make sense of. Tears pressed against the backs of her eyes. She refused to let them fall. Now wasn't the time.

Shoring up her runaway emotions, she pushed away from the door. Turning, she engaged both the deadbolt and the chain lock. Grace would sleep for another thirty minutes or so. If Peyton wanted a shower, she needed to take advantage of the moments she had. Placing the car seat near the bathroom, and leaving the door open, she quickly cleaned up. Grace had just started to stir as Peyton began to dress, and by the time she'd slipped on her sweatshirt, the baby was in a full-on tantrum.

"I'm coming... I'm coming." Peyton undid the straps

on the car seat and lifted the baby into her arms. Grace immediately quieted down, her eyes locking on Peyton's face. A crease formed between her small brows, as if she was confused. The look brought a smile to Peyton's face. "I'm your Auntie Peyton. Well... technically you and I are cousins once removed or something like that... but you can call me Auntie."

Grace's hand latched onto Peyton's finger, and her heart melted into a puddle right there. She kissed the little girl on her forehead. "I bet you're getting hungry. Let's fix a bottle."

While Peyton was figuring out the formula, she heard the faint hum of the elevator. Heavy footsteps sounded in the hallway, and then the door to a nearby room opened. Thankfully, her neighbor remained quiet. Grace, on the other hand, proved she had a healthy set of lungs. She cried and fussed no matter what Peyton tried. She fed her, burped her, rocked her, and desperately searched online for solutions to soothe her. By three a.m., the hotel room looked as if a hurricane had blown through. Half-drunk bottles, burp cloths, soiled clothes, and an assortment of toys littered the space.

Blurry-eyed and exhausted, Peyton stood in the middle of the living room, gently rocking her body side to side. The migraine that'd threatened to rear its head at the hospital had arrived. Still, she rocked on. Slowly, Grace's eyes fluttered and her breathing evened out. Peyton waited a few more minutes, and then slowly walked to the crib. Ever so gently, she laid the baby on the mattress and held her breath as Grace's eyelashes fluttered. Then the baby sighed.

On silent steps, Peyton backed away, only daring to breathe once she was across the room. She collapsed onto the bed, too tired to even pull back the covers.

A loud pounding on her door brought her to an upright position. Peyton groaned in pain as the sudden movement seemed to rock her brain inside her skull. The knocking on the door persisted. She glanced at the clock on the nightstand. 3:20 in the morning. Suddenly, worry sent a wave of adrenaline shooting through her. She grabbed her Glock from the nightstand drawer.

"Maintenance! Please open up!" The pounding on her door came again, the voice nearly panicked.

Stumbling into the living room, she shut the bedroom door in a desperate attempt to prevent the foolish individual at her door from waking up the baby. "Stop knocking." Peyton peeked through the keyhole and found a man of average height and weight wearing a hotel uniform on the other side of the door. He carried a toolbox in one hand.

Keeping her gun out of sight, she flipped open the deadbolt, but kept the chain lock in place. She opened the door a crack. "I didn't call for maintenance."

The man's face was partly hidden underneath the brim of his ball cap. His uniform was wrinkled, and a tattoo peeked out from the collar. "No, ma'am, the people below you did. Water's leaking through their ceiling from your pipes. I gotta access your bathroom to stop it."

Peyton stared at him. Her head was pounding and

her brain felt sluggish. Something about this seemed off. She didn't know much about plumbing, but how could he fix a leak downstairs by accessing her bathroom?

A cry came from the bedroom as little Grace woke up. Peyton glanced behind her.

Suddenly, she was shoved back as the man slammed into the door. The feeble chain snapped in half. Peyton raised her weapon, but the attacker was ready for it, swinging his toolbox into her arm. Agony exploded through her shoulder, and the gun dropped from her numb fingers as she cried out in pain. She stumbled back.

He lunged for the bedroom door.

"No!" Peyton threw herself at him, grabbing his jacket. He spun, intending to backhand her across the face, but she ducked. Momentum sent him crashing into the kitchen table. Cans of formula scattered. Peyton grabbed one, and with the skill she'd used on the high school softball team, flung it at his head before following up with a kick to his kidneys. He grunted in pain.

She spotted her gun on the floor and dove for it. He grabbed her foot, yanking her back before smashing a steel-toed boot into her stomach. Peyton doubled over. Through tear-filled eyes, she watched helplessly as the assailant lunged once again for the bedroom.

For Grace.

SIX

Dawson barreled down the hall and pivoted into Peyton's room with his gun raised. Grace's screams pierced the air. In a heartbeat, he took in the scene. Peyton crumpled on the floor, clutching her stomach, and a man wearing an ill-fitting hotel uniform headed for the bedroom.

"Police!" He pointed his weapon at the assailant. "Freeze!"

Dawson's finger moved to the trigger, but he couldn't take the shot—not in a hotel full of occupied rooms. A miss, or worse, a through-and-through could hit an innocent person. He crossed the room in three strides, but the attacker vaulted over the railing.

He hit the ground below—a ten-foot drop—rolled and vanished into the darkness between the buildings.

Gone.

Frustration roiled through Dawson, but the groan from Peyton behind him and Grace's continued screams set his priorities. He whirled to find Peyton struggling to sit up. Her hair tumbled loose around her shoulders, and her sweatshirt was spotted with blood. He dropped to her side. "Where are you hurt?"

"I'll... survive." Her breath came in puffs as if she'd had the wind knocked out of her. "Grace."

The baby was still wailing. Dawson went into the bedroom and found her in the crib, tiny fists and feet flailing. Other than being mighty upset, she thankfully appeared unharmed. He lifted her into his arms. "It's okay, little one. You're okay."

Grace was not convinced, her frantic cries unyielding. Dawson snagged a pacifier from the nightstand and urged the baby to take it as he carried her back into the living room. Peyton had lifted herself onto the couch and sagged against the cushions. Dark circles marred the skin under her eyes, and her complexion was pale. Seeing her like that—exhausted, fragile, and hurt—filled him with concern.

"Is she okay?" Peyton asked.

"Grace is fine." The baby finally latched onto the pacifier and quieted down. Dawson called the incident in. Dispatch promised to send officers right away. He hung up and focused back on Peyton. "What happened?"

She rubbed her temple as if her head was aching. "I was stupid. He came to the door, demanding to be let in. Something about a leak in the room below me. It didn't sit right, and I was just about to close the door and call the front desk when he shoved his way in." Her hazel eyes were filled with concern and pain. "He wanted Grace. He kept trying to get into the bedroom."

Dawson scanned the small space. He spotted a bottle of over-the-counter medication next to the sink. Lifting Grace to his shoulder, he retrieved two pills and filled a glass of water. He handed them to Peyton. "Take these."

She ignored his outstretched hand. "Did you hear me? He came here for Grace."

"I'm not deaf. Now take the medication, Peyton, before you pass out from the pain." He waited, and when she stayed still, sighed. "Please. You can't help anyone if you don't take care of yourself."

She took the medication and drank the water. "It's annoying when you're right."

His mouth quirked. "I know." Dawson eyed the coffee table, and after deciding it would support his weight, perched on the edge. It creaked in protest. He reached out, his fingers gentle as he lifted a lock of her hair away from her face. A cut marred her jaw. It didn't appear deep, but it had bled enough to stain her throat and her sweatshirt. His thumb hovered near the wound, close enough to feel her warmth but not close enough to touch.

He gritted his teeth and mentally swore that the men who'd dared to lay hands on her would be brought to justice. He'd make sure of it. "Did you get a good look at the attacker? Enough to ID him?"

"Yes." Peyton moved away from his touch, using the corner of the blanket to wipe the tear tracks from Grace's cheeks. "Caucasian male, 5′10 and 180 pounds. Brown hair, brown eyes. Had a tattoo on his neck—couldn't make out what it was—but the top was blue and red. And he was wearing steel-toed boots."

She gestured toward the plastic toolbox on the ground. "He carried that. Forensics might get prints." Irritation made her nostrils flare. "I can't believe he got the drop on me. That's the second time in 24 hours I've been disarmed, and you best believe, there won't be a third."

"Calm down there, tiger. You're dealing with a concussion and enough bruises to leave a boxer down for the count."

"Still... I'm a law enforcement officer. I know better. If you hadn't shown up when you did..." Peyton paused. "Wait a second, what are you doing here? How..." Her gaze narrowed. "You never left the hotel after dropping us off, did you?"

That it took her so long to put two and two together was a testament to how much pain she was in. "No. I rented the room next door. It was the best way to make sure you and Grace were safe." Dawson had hoped he was wrong about his suspicions, but after this second attack, there were no doubts. "Whatever trouble Lilia was in, it's now on your doorstep, and we need to make a plan."

"What kind of plan?"

He couldn't believe he was about to suggest this. "You and Grace should come stay with my family. The ranch is secure, and my parents can help care for Grace while you recover from your injuries." He met her gaze, already sensing her resistance. "You're exhausted, overwhelmed, and hurt. There's no shame in accepting my help."

She was silent for a long moment. "I can't keep leaning on you, Dawson. It's not fair. To either of us. Things are different now."

"You're right. They are. You made sure of it."

Silence hung heavy between them after his harsh words. He could feel it, rolling just under the cap of his control. That pent-up anger and sadness about the way things ended between them. After Samuel's death, he'd done everything he could to hold them together. He'd been patient. Loving. A rock she could hold on to in the storm of her grief.

Instead, Peyton had just drifted further and further away. She refused any offer of help. Counseling. Church. Everything he did made her mad. She lashed out. Then fell into silence. Until that final day, at the kitchen table, when she announced the decision to get divorced.

Ten years of being in love. Three years of marriage. Over. Just... done.

He'd deserved better. Dawson knew that. And here was another chance to walk away from this situation. But he couldn't. It wasn't in his DNA. Peyton had been his wife. He'd stood in a church and promised before God to honor and cherish her. They were not vows he took lightly. Dawson wasn't interested in repairing their marriage—that was dead and buried—but he also couldn't pretend Peyton meant nothing to him. She was in danger. Grace too. The best way to protect them both was on his family's ranch, behind surveillance cameras and armed ranch hands.

Dawson drew in a breath and tempered his tone. "Things are different between us now, Peyton, but these aren't normal circumstances. You need help. I can provide it." He paused, struggling to put what he was feeling into words. "Before we were together as a couple, we were friends, and I know if the roles were reversed, you'd do the same for me."

A knock on the door interrupted their conversation.

"Knoxville Police Department." The voice was authoritative.

Dawson handed Grace off to Peyton before crossing the room and peeking through the keyhole. Officer Tucker Colburn stood in the hall. Dawson opened the door and greeted his colleague.

A former Army Ranger, Tucker's auburn hair was shorn in a military-style haircut, and his sharp-eyed gaze missed nothing. He took in the formula cans scattered on the floor, Peyton's injuries, and the tension in Dawson's stance with the practiced efficiency of a soldier assessing a battlefield. "Everyone okay? Should I call for the paramedics?"

"Yes," Dawson said.

"No," Peyton replied at the same moment.

Tucker's brows raised, and he shot a questioning glance at Dawson, who shook his head in exasperation. If Peyton wanted to refuse medical attention, he couldn't force her. Instead, he focused on what he could control. The case. He ran through the attack and then led Tucker to the balcony. "The assailant went that way." Dawson pointed to the alley between the buildings. "You should conduct a grid search for evidence. And call Liam. He's the primary investigator on this case. He'll probably want to take Peyton's statement himself."

The next few hours were spent handling the monotonous details of an investigation. Cataloging evidence, questioning witnesses, and photographing the scene. Dawson stood on the balcony and watched as the sun came up over the freeway as officers swept the property. Peyton and Grace were napping in the bedroom.

The sliding glass door opened behind him. A moment later, Detective Jax Taylor appeared by his side, holding a couple of to-go coffees.

Surprise flickered through Dawson. Jax was supposed to be in Louisiana helping his cousin move to Knoxville. "Aren't you on vacation?"

"Not anymore." He handed a coffee to Dawson. "I heard about the attack last night and drove back."

"Come on, man. You didn't have to do that." Dawson accepted the coffee and leveled a look at his friend. "What about your cousin? Did you just bail on him?"

"Nope. He had friends from college helping him . And before you start feeling guilty, I didn't just rush back because of you. I missed Megan."

Dawson had no doubt there was truth in that last statement. Since solving his brother's murder case and falling in love with Megan, Jax had become... lighter. Hopeful about the future. It was nice to see. And while Dawson would never admit it out loud, he was relieved to see his old friend. They'd been buddies since elementary school, and there was no one who knew him better.

He took a sip of the coffee and let the caffeine jolt his tired brain into action. "How much did Liam tell you?"

Liam was the only one who would've called Jax. His colleague was quiet, but nothing escaped his notice. Dawson had sensed Liam understood the complicated undercurrents running between Dawson and Peyton. He probably hadn't intended for Jax to return from his vacation, but had called to get his opinion.

Something Dawson would deal with later. Liam had meant well, but he should've just asked Dawson directly.

"He gave me the basics." Jax mirrored Dawson's posture, leaning on the railing. "I'd hoped the attack on Peyton at the train depot was a one-off or some kind of mistake, but this second assault leaves no question. She's being targeted."

"Actually, the intruder was after the baby. Although it's unclear why." Dawson turned the cup in his hands. "The birth certificate doesn't list a father. Maybe he's involved somehow. Whoever is behind this was smart enough to figure out which hotel Peyton was staying at and in which room. Most criminals wouldn't go to all that trouble. And most won't dare to touch a law enforcement officer. They don't want that kind of heat. This feels personal."

"I agree. There's no sign of Lilia yet."

Dawson's stomach tightened. He didn't want to imagine the worst, but with every passing hour, it became a higher probability that they wouldn't find Peyton's cousin alive. "Did Liam find the homeless guy Peyton mentioned at the hospital?"

"We did a sweep but didn't find him. Most of the people staying at the depot probably scattered at the sound of police sirens." Jax adjusted his cowboy hat on his head. "After we finish up here, we're doing another search of the area around the train depot. And I'm going with Liam to interview Lilia's mom. Hopefully, we'll have more answers in a few hours."

Dawson prayed he was right.

"In the meantime, we should move Peyton and Grace to another hotel," Jax continued. "Put them under a pseudonym. We can't spare any officers to stand guard, but I'll have patrols make frequent drive-bys."

The Knoxville Police Department was small and their resources limited. It was the reason Dawson had offered to have Peyton stay on his ranch. "She and Grace may come to stay with my family. I'll let you know."

Jax's gaze narrowed. "You don't need me to tell you that's a bad idea."

Dawson stared across the parking lot, letting his gaze lift to the highway and then the sky. It was painted with hues of the sunrise. Jax's concern settled over him like a wet blanket—heavy and harder to shrug off than he wanted. "I have to do this. She doesn't have anyone else."

"That's not your responsibility anymore." Jax's voice was gentle now, almost sad. "She made that choice when she left."

The words stung because they were true.

"I'm worried about you. Losing Peyton nearly destroyed you last time."

Dawson was touched by his friend's concern. And it wasn't unwarranted. But he'd also had a lot of time to think last night. "Walking away like she did... there's no coming back from that. Our marriage is done. I could never fully trust her again. But Peyton also apologized last night at the hospital for the way things ended between us." It was hard to explain unless someone had been through it. The loss of a child. It changed you in ways that couldn't be put into words. "We were both grieving and not ourselves. And... I don't know. She reached for help, and yes, I could turn her away. Or I could use this as an opportunity to say goodbye the right way and finally close this chapter of my life."

"Do you think you can do that? Say goodbye the right way?"

"I think it's worth a try. We had fifteen years together, most of it good." Dawson twisted the coffee cup in his hand. "It took a lot of work to pick up the pieces after she left, and I've rebuilt a life I'm proud of, but even I have to admit that a part of me is stuck."

He'd tried dating here and there, but never seriously. Dawson had made excuses for it, but Peyton's sudden reappearance in his life made the real reason impossible to ignore. He hadn't let her go. Not fully. But he needed to, and now was the chance.

From the expression on Jax's face, he doubted the wisdom of this plan and was trying to figure out the best way to say so. Dawson didn't need to hear it.

"I know what I'm doing." He took a sip of his coffee. "Besides, this is the best solution for everyone. We need every available officer looking for Lilia and the attackers. Now, more than ever."

Jax blew out a breath. "Well... can't say I didn't try."

Dawson chuckled and clapped him on the shoulder. "A for effort."

"Yeah, but an F for results."

They both laughed at that. Jax left to help with the search for evidence. A few moments later, Peyton appeared, her hair mussed from the pillow, Grace in her arms. The baby wriggled and fussed. She was a sweet little thing, but in the last few hours, she'd only slept in thirty-minute bursts. It was difficult to know if she was colicky, or the uproar in her life had unsettled her. Either way, she was wearing Peyton down. The dark circles had abated somewhat, but Peyton still looked like a stiff wind could blow her over.

Dawson stepped forward, handing over his half-filled cup and reaching for Grace. "I'll take the baby. You drink that."

Peyton didn't argue. She took a long sip of the coffee and sighed. "Oh, that's good." She breathed in the crisp morning air, and a faint smile lifted her lips as she tipped her face toward the sky. Birds twittered from a nearby pine tree.

Dawson's breath caught. She was beautiful like this. Hair mussed, face soft in the morning light, that small smile playing at her lips. The last five years had added a faint scar along her jawline and loosened some waves in her hair. There were also intangible differences. A quiet steadiness that had never existed before, a stillness... almost... a peace?

He tore his gaze away and busied himself with adjusting Grace's blanket. It was pink with stars dancing across it. The baby whimpered from behind her pacifier, so he swayed rhythmically, hoping it would keep her content. An idea formed. He pulled the keys from his pocket and undid the clip holding Grace's pacifier to her shirt.

"What are you doing?" Peyton asked.

"Giving us an advantage. Here... hold Grace for a second." He passed the baby back to her before removing the GPS tracker on his key ring. He attached it to Grace using the pacifier clip, tucking it between the layers of her clothing so it wasn't visible to the naked eye. "There. If, in the unlikely event, someone grabs Grace, we'll be able to track her on my phone."

"That's brilliant." Peyton smiled up at him.

"It's not perfect, but it's better than nothing." Dawson took Grace back so Peyton could drink her coffee while he filled her in on the little they knew.

Peyton asked a few questions, but then fell into silence, fiddling with the carton sleeve on the coffee cup. "How did it come to this? Lilia has stumbled into trouble, but never anything this serious."

Dawson had no answer for that.

She sighed. "I've been thinking about your offer. To stay on the ranch."

"And?"

"It's generous of you to help, but are you sure you want to do this? Will your family be okay with me being there?" She let her gaze drift over the grounds. "I wouldn't blame any of you if you hated me. I hurt you, Dawson, and I'm sorry for that. I'm sorry... for a lot of things."

A sadness swept over him, along with compassion for the pain trembling in her voice. "No one in my family hates you. And I don't either. But if you're uncomfortable staying at the ranch, Jax said Knoxville PD can set you up in a hotel under a fake name. The choice is yours."

She bit her lip, and then her gaze went to the baby in his arms. Her shoulders dropped, as if the tension in her muscles had finally eased. She nodded. "Okay. I'll go pack our stuff."

The knot of worry in his stomach loosened. "Sounds good."

Peyton turned toward the sliding door and then stopped. She glanced over her shoulder. "Dawson, you should know, I've thought about calling you hundreds of times. I didn't because... well, it seemed unfair after what I did. But if you're ever ready to talk, I'd like to."

The words landed somewhere deep in his chest. There was a lot he wanted to say too—questions he'd never gotten answers to, hurt he'd never fully voiced. But now wasn't the time. "Let's focus on finding Lilia and protecting Grace. After that, we'll see."

She nodded and slipped inside the hotel, leaving the faint scent of jasmine in her wake.

Dawson lifted his gaze to the sky. *Okay, God, I'm not sure where you're leading me, but I'm trusting You.*

SEVEN

Morning sunshine streamed through the gauzy curtains covering the window. Awareness came slowly as Peyton swam up from a deep sleep. The soft bed and thick comforter were so cozy, she was tempted to keep her eyes closed and drift back off, but the scent of coffee and the faint sound of a door slamming somewhere in the house pulled her to full consciousness. With regret, she rolled over to check the time on her cell phone.

And immediately sat straight up. Nine thirty. She'd slept for over twelve hours.

Grace. She looked toward the crib set up in the corner of the room. It was empty, save for a discarded blanket. Someone—likely Dawson or his mom—must've come in and taken the baby while she was sleeping. Peyton kicked off the covers and went into the adjoining bathroom to clean up before heading toward the sound of voices coming from the kitchen.

"Good morning!" Ellen Graham, Dawson's mother,

flashed a bright smile from the other side of the island covered in sugar cookies. In one hand, she wielded an icing bag, and the other rested against the soft cloth wrapped snugly around her chest. Her brown hair was streaked with gorgeous silver strands that brought out the brightness of her cerulean eyes. A cup of coffee rested nearby. "Did you sleep well? There's fresh coffee."

"I slept very well. Too well. I didn't hear Grace wake at all." Her gaze scanned the kitchen for any sign of her ward. "Where is she?"

"Right here." Ellen tilted slightly, and Grace's wild curls came into view, nestled against Ellen's chest in the folds of the wrap. The baby's eyes were closed in bliss, her little mouth moving against the pacifier absently. "She loves the sling. I found it's the best way to get her to sleep."

Peyton smiled and gently brushed a soft curl away from Grace's rosy cheek. "What time did you take her out of my room?"

A flash of guilt creased Ellen's features. "About thirty minutes after you went to bed. Maybe I shouldn't have, but you looked so tired, hon, and it was clear Grace has a touch of colic."

Peyton remembered all too well staying up most of the night with a screaming baby. "I hope she wasn't too much trouble."

"Not at all. I love having babies around, and being able to take care of Grace is such a blessing. She's a sweetheart." Ellen winked. "She's got everyone wrapped around her finger already. Raymond was up with her at dawn, and Dawson insisted on giving her a morning bottle. I think you might have to fight us all in order to get a second with her, and that's before the rest of the family sees her."

Peyton laughed and poured herself a cup of coffee. "From what I hear, Claire and Marcus have their hands full already."

Ellen chuckled and went back to icing her cookie. "They do, but don't let them fool you. They're enjoying every minute. And so am I. Having all these grandkids underfoot is wonderful. The laughter, the crying, and the glitter."

Peyton smiled. "It sounds wonderful." A pang of sadness hit her. Samuel should be here with them. He'd be nearly five now, running through the house wearing a cape and begging for a cookie from his grandmother. Not a day went by that she didn't think of him, but somehow, the loss was more poignant standing in this familiar kitchen with its ancient cabinets and the rooster clock hanging above the doorway.

Maybe coming to the ranch had been a mistake. But what choice did she have? The attack yesterday proved Grace was in danger, and above all else, it was Peyton's job to protect her.

The back door opened, and her heart pitched as the low rumble of Dawson's voice reached her ears. A moment later, he appeared in the kitchen, dressed in ranch clothes. Worn work jeans, a flannel over a T-shirt, and a silver belt buckle. He'd removed his boots, but even in stocking feet, his presence made an impact. He brought with him the scent of fresh air and a hint of hay. She breathed it in, letting it soothe her.

His brown eyes met hers, and he smiled. "Look who's finally up." His gaze swept over her, and Peyton felt him cataloging her features. "How do you feel?"

"Much better." The sleep had erased her headache and most of her muscle soreness.

Raymond Graham entered the kitchen. Dawson's father was as tall as his son, and just as wide. His jet-black hair held a tinge of gray, but his dark skin was unlined. He greeted his wife with a kiss on her cheek before heading to the coffee machine. "We mended the broken fence in the back fifty, but the Sutters across the street have a fallen tree on their shed. They're still in Florida visiting their daughter until the end of the week, so I'll take my chainsaw over this afternoon and handle it."

The Sutters were in their seventies and had been neighbors with the Grahams for decades. For as long as Peyton had known them, Ellen and Raymond had cooked, cleaned, and helped care for their property. That was who they were. They helped everyone who needed it. When Raymond became assistant pastor of the local church, the demands on their time increased. It was a lot to keep up with the ranch and serve their community, but Peyton had never heard them complain once.

"Is there any news about Lilia?" she asked Dawson.

He shook his head, and the flare of hope she'd allowed herself to feel died. Her cousin had been missing for over 24 hours.

"We're all praying for Lilia." Raymond rested a giant hand on Peyton's shoulder. "Not just us, but the whole church. Chief Garcia was on the local news last night asking for leads. I know everyone in town will keep an eye out." He kissed the top of her head as if she was one of his own children, and the tender move sent another wave of aching nostalgia through her. Despite her reservations about seeing the Grahams again, they had been nothing but supportive and loving from the moment she'd arrived yesterday morning.

As if nothing had changed. As if she hadn't divorced their son.

As if she were still family.

Several phones chimed at once. Raymond removed his cell from his pocket and grinned. "Uh-oh. Incoming."

Peyton's brow crinkled as she glanced at Dawson. "What does that mean?"

He chuckled. "You'll see."

Moments later, the back door swung open with the force of a hurricane. "Grandma!" Feet beat against the tile seconds before two curly-haired kids streaked into the kitchen. The room dissolved into chaos, as kisses and hugs were exchanged, and the kids asked a million questions. Marcus, Dawson's younger brother, appeared in the doorway. He looked rumpled. His hair stuck up in different directions, and his shirt was misbuttoned. He had a baby carrier slung over one arm and a thick bag hooked on one shoulder.

"Here, let me help you, son." Raymond took the baby

carrier from him. Nestled inside was a little girl, roughly the same age as Grace.

"Thanks, Dad." Marcus collapsed into the nearest chair. Oliver, a chubby-cheeked little boy of around two, instantly climbed into his dad's lap and started reaching for a muffin from a stack on the table. His dad ignored him. "Someone get me some coffee, please."

Dawson obliged, setting a mug in front of his brother with a grin. "You okay there, baby brother?"

"Jessica is running on fumes, so I thought it would be a good idea to take the kids this morning by myself so she can rest." He sucked down the coffee in a huge gulp. "I'm outnumbered and outsmarted. Before I could even get them dressed, Izzy colored on the walls and Oliver spilled an entire box of cereal on the floor."

Dawson chuckled and scooped up Oliver into his broad arms, muffin and all. The little boy had a bit of a runny nose, so he gently wiped it with a napkin before settling him in a highchair. Peyton's heart squeezed tight. And then her breath caught when Dawson grabbed her hand. "Come on. Let's escape the chaos. There's something I want to discuss with you."

She dragged her feet. "What about Grace?"

Dawson leaned closer to Peyton. "Mom will never give you that baby back, you know that, right?" His whispered voice was purposefully loud enough for his mother to hear. She threw a potholder his way. It bounced off his massive chest and fell to the floor. He picked it up, laughing. "Don't be mad at me for speaking the truth, Mom."

Ellen's eyes sparkled with love and laughter. "You're

a troublemaker, that's what you are." Her voice was warm with affection. Then she turned to Peyton. "I promise I will give her back." She paused. "Eventually."

Peyton giggled. She realized as she stepped out onto the front porch, bundled in a jacket, that she'd somehow slid right back into her place on the ranch. Sunshine spilled over the grass. The fields were enclosed with white picket fences and horses grazed near the country road leading to the property. It was picturesque and peaceful. She drew in a breath and let it out slowly, stealing one last moment for herself before the weight of it all returned.

Dawson joined her at the railing. He'd lingered in the kitchen long enough to pour his own cup of coffee. Steam drifted up from the dark brew into the frigid air. The easy expression he'd worn in the kitchen was gone, replaced by a furrow of worry on his brow. That, more than anything, sent Peyton's heart skittering. She felt a momentary bite of fear. "What aren't you telling me? Is it Lilia?"

"No, there's been no sign of her." Dawson turned and leaned against the railing. It creaked under his weight, and Peyton wondered if the wood—worn from generations of use—would give out from underneath him. "But there are two pieces of news. First, you were right about the fingerprints on the toolbox."

He pulled out his cell phone and tapped on the screen, pulling up a photograph. Peyton stepped closer to view it. The warmth of his body bled through her jacket, and her pulse responded before her brain could intervene. She pressed her lips together and forced herself to focus on the image. A man stared back at her. Lanky with dirty dark hair and a calculating gaze. A tattoo peeked out from the corner of his collar.

She stiffened. "That's the guy from the hotel."

"Marvis Harrison."

The name wasn't familiar. "Has he been arrested?"

"Not yet. A BOLO has been issued for him, but so far, he hasn't been seen since he escaped after the attack. His last known address is Waco. He's got a long rap sheet, including a second-degree murder charge, but he's never done any serious prison time. The cases were all plead down or dismissed."

She frowned. "What's his connection to Lilia?"

"We don't know. Waco PD went to his last known address, but his mother claimed to not know where he was. She kicked him out last year and hasn't seen him since. He doesn't have any ties to Knoxville that we know of. His mother said he owns a motorcycle though."

"So he could be a member of the Iron Serpents?"

"Maybe."

Peyton took that in. Now that her concussion had faded, and she'd had adequate sleep, her brain finally felt like it was working again. "There were two guys at the train depot. If we assume Marvis was one of them, it doesn't explain who the other one was. Or why anyone in the Iron Serpents would be after Grace." She turned the thought over. Dread gripped her. "Marvis could be Grace's father. Or whoever he's working with could be."

"It's definitely possible."

"Has anyone interviewed my Aunt Sandra? What did she have to say?"

"That's the other thing I wanted to share with you. Sandra refused to talk to Jax and Liam."

Peyton was incredulous. "They explained that Lilia's life was in danger?"

Dawson's jaw tightened. "They did. But she's suspicious and doesn't believe Liam and Jax are trustworthy."

She scoffed. "Of course not. They're cops." Sandra had plenty of run-ins with the police, and none of them had been good. Peyton immediately knew what she had to do. "I'll speak to her. Convince her to help us."

"You're not going alone."

For heaven's sake, she was a Special Agent. She could handle one conversation with her aunt. And while she appreciated all the things Dawson had done for her, every minute in his presence was making it harder and harder to keep those walls up around her heart. "Dawson, I appreciate the help—"

He held up a hand. "Don't even try. We have no idea what these guys are after, or why. You've been attacked twice now, and I won't give them a third chance."

"In both cases, Grace was the target."

"Yeah, well, that doesn't mean it'll remain that way."

EIGHT

The trailer sat at the end of the country dirt road, rutted with potholes and debris. Peyton's stomach tightened in a familiar knot as Dawson eased the SUV past a sagging mailbox, the name Morrison still visible in faded paint. The half-acre lot had once belonged to Nana Grace, inherited from her husband, and then gifted to Sandra back when she still believed her youngest daughter would get clean, settle down, and build a life worth having.

Honestly, Peyton was surprised Sandra hadn't sold the property years ago. It was worth more than everything else her aunt owned combined. Maybe, in some small, buried corner of her heart, Sandra held on to it because it was the last thing her mother had given her. Or maybe she'd just been too drunk to think of it.

Dawson parked near a rusted pickup truck with two flat tires and weeds growing through the wheel wells. A collection of garbage bags sat piled near the front steps, some torn open by animals. The trailer's siding was streaked with mildew, and a window on the far end was patched with cardboard and duct tape.

She remembered this place differently. Not fondly— it had never been well-kept—but there'd been a time when Nana Grace mowed the grass, planted flowers along the walkway, and scrubbed the porch. She'd done it without complaint or expectation of thanks, because that was Nana Grace. She tended things. Even things that didn't want to be tended.

The flowers were long dead. The walkway had disappeared under a tangle of crabgrass. And the porch sagged under the weight of neglect and time.

"You ready to do this?" Dawson's hand came to rest on her arm. His touch was gentle, and when Peyton turned to face him, she saw empathy reflected in the depths of his dark eyes. He knew everything. The whole difficult history. She didn't have to explain why her muscles were tense or why she hadn't moved to open the door. He just knew.

It was more comforting than she wanted to admit.

"No." Peyton had to battle the urge to tell Dawson to hit reverse and take them out of here. She'd tried for years to rescue Lilia from the clutches of her mother's destructive ways, and felt crushing hopelessness every time her cousin inevitably ended up right back at the trailer. It'd caused more than one argument, and then eventually a rift. One Nana Grace had never agreed with. She'd urged the girls to have patience and love for one another.

If she were alive, her grandmother would be sorely

disappointed in Peyton's actions. In the three years of silence she'd allowed between herself and Lilia. She owed it to her cousin to see if Sandra had information that could help them. "But I don't have a choice, so let's get it done."

She reached for the door before she could talk herself out of it. Then paused. "Thanks for coming with me, Dawson. I'm glad I don't have to do this alone."

His mouth turned up into an endearing smile. "Does that mean you'll stop arguing with me?"

"I wouldn't go that far."

His chuckle followed her out of the vehicle. The grass clawed at her boots, and the frigid wind whipped her hair. She paused long enough to grab the bag of groceries they'd stopped to buy along the way before heading for the trailer. Dawson followed a step behind.

The door to the trailer opened. Sandra stepped out, wearing a tattered bathrobe and two different slippers. Time and alcohol had ravaged her. She looked waif-thin, with deep hollows beneath her cheekbones. She clutched a mug in one hand. Sympathy stirred in Peyton despite everything. She knew her aunt suffered from addiction, that she needed help, but Sandra had abused the many opportunities offered to her. To make matters worse, she was a mean drunk. Even now, her watery eyes narrowed with calculation and nastiness.

"Look at what the cat dragged in." Sandra's voice was rough, as if she'd been smoking a pack of cigarettes for breakfast. "I must've won the lottery or something if Princess Peyton is here slumming it with the likes of me."

She ignored the insult. "Hi, Aunt Sandra." Peyton shifted the grocery sack. "We brought food. Mind if we come inside? I need to speak to you. It's important."

"Food, huh? What kind?"

Peyton listed a few items. Sandra's expression soured with obvious disappointment. "You didn't bring anything to drink, did you?"

"There's orange juice in the bag."

Sandra scoffed. "That's not what I meant, and you know it." Her gaze slid to Dawson, sizing him up before dismissing him and focusing back on Peyton. She sniffed. "At least Lilia knew how to show up properly."

The implication stung. Lilia had bought her mother's attention with bottles and cigarettes for years. It was something Peyton and her cousin had argued about most bitterly. Enabling Sandra wasn't love. It was surrender. But standing on this rotting porch with her aunt's blood-shot eyes boring into her, Peyton understood the tempta-tion. It would've been so much easier.

"I've got food and coffee," Peyton said evenly. "And questions about your daughter. Can we come in? It's freezing out here."

"Suit yourself."

She led the way inside. Dimly lit, the interior of the trailer was barely warmer than the outdoors. Threadbare carpet covered the living room, ending at the torn linoleum floor in the kitchen. A roach the size of her thumb scampered down the hall toward the closed bedroom door. Peyton shuddered. She struggled to find a clean spot on the counter to place the groceries among the empty bottles of booze and takeaway cartons. Moldy dishes sat in dirty dishwater. She nearly gagged.

"Give it to me." Dawson tugged the bag from Peyton's hand. His voice was low and non-judgmental. "Go talk to your aunt."

Embarrassment heated the back of her neck. Dawson understood her aunt's troubles, but it was still humiliating for him to see it firsthand. Especially after the warmth and happiness of his own family's kitchen. Unable to meet his gaze, she fished out a ready-made sandwich before heading into the living room.

Sandra had settled herself on a broken recliner, a cigarette already in hand. A half-empty bottle of cheap bourbon rested on the coffee table. She gestured to it. "Pour me a drink, Princess Peyton. Might as well make yourself useful while you're here."

"I've got a better idea." She offered the sandwich. "You might feel better if you eat something."

"I'm fine." Sandra grabbed the sandwich and tossed it on the table before grabbing the bourbon bottle. The liquid sloshed into her broken mug. "You always were a judgy thing. You think I don't feel it? Your disgust. You always thought you were better than me and my daughter. And I told Lilia so time and time again."

Peyton ignored the attempt to get a rise out of her. It was an old argument. She was tempted to continue standing for their discussion, but decided against it, perching instead on the stained couch. "When was the last time you saw Lilia?"

The sound of running water punctuated her question. Likely Dawson doing the dishes. Peyton had been wise enough to add some cleaning supplies to the grocery order. She wanted to tell him to stop—that it wasn't necessary—but didn't have the emotional energy to deal with it.

Sandra took a long sip of her drink before puffing away on her cigarette. "It's been a minute." She eyed Peyton with suspicion. "Is she in some kind of trouble? Them other cops came here, asking me the same question. Tried to trick me into talkin' to 'em by telling me my girl was missing."

"She is missing." Peyton planted her hands on her knees. "She called me two days ago. Said she was in trouble and begged me to meet her. When I arrived, I heard her scream. I was attacked. Shot at. The two men who came at me escaped, and we don't know where Lilia is." She looked at her aunt, letting all the urgency and worry plaguing her seep into her voice. "She's in danger, and Aunt Sandra, I need your help to find her."

Sandra blinked, as if her brain were processing the news slowly through the haze of alcohol. Then her mouth curled into a sneer. "You're lying."

"I wouldn't lie about something like this."

"Unless you were looking to arrest my Lilia and throw her in jail for something." Sandra jabbed her cigarette toward Peyton, and ashes tumbled to the nasty carpet. "You can't trick me."

"This isn't a trick!" Peyton's voice rose as the hold on her temper snapped. She closed her eyes, frustrated with herself. Her aunt needed compassion, but she made it so difficult. Peyton silently asked the Lord for patience and then focused back on Sandra. "This isn't a game. Or a lie. I'm deadly serious. Lilia's life is in danger, and if you love her at all, then you'll stop giving me the runaround and start talking."

Her tone was sharp and unyielding, and there must've been something in her expression that convinced Sandra, because her gray complexion paled. Peyton nodded, as if confirming her aunt's silent question. "Now, I'll ask again, when was the last time you saw Lilia?"

"I dunno. It's been a while."

The days ran together for her aunt. Peyton tried a different tack. "Are we talking weeks or months? Summer? Winter?"

Sandra seemed to consider the question. "Winter." She took another sip of her bourbon, but this time, her hand trembled. "It was cold, like today. Like I said, it's been a while."

So a year ago? It seemed like a logical assumption. "Okay. Can you remember what happened?"

Now it was her aunt's turn to glower. "I'm not an idiot. Of course, I can remember. She popped in for a quick visit. Said she was going away for a while, but I shouldn't worry."

Dread churned Peyton's insides. "Going away where?"

"Don't know."

Peyton let the silence stretch between them, hoping her aunt would say more. Sandra stayed stubbornly silent. She could be sly when necessary. "Lilia didn't mention where she was going? Or for how long?"

"Nope."

She had the nagging suspicion her aunt wasn't being fully honest, but didn't know how to pinpoint what she was lying about. She took a different tack. "Does Lilia have any connection to the Iron Serpents?"

Sandra considered the question through a haze of smoke. "She was hanging out with Cade Maddox." She dissolved into a cough that sounded wet before choking out, "He's a big shot with the Iron Serpents, so I hear."

The name rang a distant bell. Peyton's gaze snapped to Dawson, who gave a sharp nod of agreement. The fridge door hung open behind him. He'd moved on from the dishes to putting the food away. He looked so out of place there in the depressing and dirty kitchen.

She'd done that. Dragged him into this awful mess. Peyton should've known he wouldn't let her face this alone, just as she knew he'd have everything put in order in the kitchen before this interview was done. That was who he was. So much like Nana Grace. No wonder her grandmother had loved him so.

She focused back on Sandra. "How long were Lilia and Cade dating?"

"Which time?"

"They dated more than once?"

"Yep. Lilia was crazy about Cade. Back then, he was just a little twerp selling pot to get by, but he convinced her to drop out of high school and run away with him to

Vegas. Cade liked to play poker, and he won big when he had Lilia there to count the cards."

Pride edged into her voice. Lilia was a mathematical genius. Sandra had always felt her daughter's talents directly resulted from her mothering. Nothing could be farther from the truth.

"I thought for sure they'd get married, but she came back three months later, licking her wounds, crying about how you can't trust a man." Sandra sucked down what was in her coffee mug and then poured herself another drink. "I figured he'd lost big gambling, drained her bank account, and left her to fend for herself."

Peyton remembered the incident. Nana Grace had been worried sick, and Peyton had nearly left college and gotten on a plane to go hunt down her cousin. Lilia's reappearance in Knoxville had stopped her. She'd chalked it up to another one of her cousin's stunts. They'd argued over it, mostly over how Lilia had treated Nana Grace and caused her untold amounts of stress.

"It was Cade she ran off with?" Peyton stared at the carpet and let the memories roll over her. She'd met this guy. Once during a Sunday dinner while visiting on spring break. She'd been in college. Nearly ten years ago. He'd been dressed all in black and had a motorcycle. What she remembered most was the fact that he'd been high. Peyton had gotten through dinner, but when he toppled over the dessert tray after two bottles of wine, she'd told him to leave. That hadn't earned her any points with Lilia. Another thing they'd fought about.

It was hard to imagine that same man was now helping to run a sophisticated criminal organization.

Could Cade be Grace's father? It was an upsetting thought.

Peyton shifted uncomfortably on the couch. She could feel the old springs digging into her backside. "When you saw Lilia last, did she say anything about being pregnant?"

"No. A'course Lilia knows my feelings about that. Kids do nothing but drag you down. Better to get rid of them and be done with it." Sandra seemed oblivious to the fact that she'd treated her own daughter like a disposable tissue. Useful when she needed her, but otherwise, something she could throw away without any regard. "And Cade never struck me as someone who wanted to be a daddy."

Laughter bubbled up in Sandra's throat and she choked on it again, nearly doubling over with the effort to pull air into her lungs. "He's a good-time guy." She wheezed, her face red. "If Lilia got pregnant, he'd dump her quick."

"You seem to know a lot about Cade."

"I know a lot about men. Especially his kind."

Peyton couldn't argue with that. Her aunt had had her fair share of failed relationships. "Where was Lilia living?"

"Don't know. Don't care." Sandra struggled to ignite the lighter for her next cigarette. "I don't ask her a whole lotta questions. I've got my own issues to worry about."

"Right." Peyton resisted the urge to roll her eyes. "If

Lilia was in trouble, is there someplace you can think of that she'd hide out? Or someone she'd turn to for help?"

"Other than you? Nope."

A creak came from the rear of the trailer. Peyton was on her feet in an instant. "Who else is here?"

"Bobby. My man." Sandra glared from underneath thin eyebrows. "What's the matter with you? You think I'm too old to have someone who cares about me."

The bedroom door swung open and an overweight, balding man filled the hallway. He wore sweatpants with frayed holes and a stained white tank top. Tattoos covered much of his visible skin. Several were associated with known prison gangs. His gaze widened with surprise as Dawson stepped out of the kitchen.

"Hey, man." Dawson's posture was casual, but he strategically placed himself between Bobby and Peyton in a protective stance.

"What's going on?" Bobby demanded. His expression reddened as his anger sparked. "What ya' doing talking with cops, Sandra?"

"Aw, Bobby, don't get riled up. This is my niece. She's here about Lilia. She thinks my daughter might be in some kind of trouble." Sandra's tone was sugary sweet. "You ain't got nothin' to worry about, hon."

Bobby didn't look convinced. "I'm sure Lilia is fine." He puffed out his chest, stepping forward aggressively. "Visiting time is over. Get out."

There wasn't any love lost between Peyton and her aunt, but even still, she couldn't leave the older woman with Bobby in good conscience. The man looked ready to punch someone, and he'd literally just woken up. His hair was mussed and there was a crease on his cheek from the pillow.

She eased closer to Sandra. Keeping her voice low, she whispered, "This is your house, Aunt Sandra. If you're afraid, I can help you."

Sandra met her gaze. Some of that hardened shell she wore cracked, and a weariness swam in her dark eyes. "Bobby takes care of me."

That was code for he kept her in alcohol and cigarettes. Maybe drugs too. Peyton touched her aunt's arm. It was nothing but bone. "It doesn't have to be this way."

"Aw, Princess Peyton. What do you know of life?" Her gaze hardened, the weariness disappearing behind a lifetime of regret and anger. Her voice rose. "You heard Bobby. Get out."

Knowing she wouldn't make any progress, Peyton reluctantly headed for the door, Dawson hot on her heels. The slap of fresh air was a relief after the sourness of the trailer. She practically ran down the sagging porch steps to the SUV.

Moments later, icy air washed into the cab. Peyton had opened the window, unable to clear the stench from her nose. She needed a shower. Pine trees whipped by.

"We should figure out Bobby's last name and run him through the system." Peyton had to shout to be heard over the wind. "I'll eat my badge if he doesn't have a criminal record."

Dawson nodded. "You think he's involved in Lilia's disappearance?"

"Everyone is a suspect until we know otherwise, and he seemed pretty ticked off to find us there." The air had turned strands of her hair into whips, so she gave in and pulled up the window halfway. "Not to mention that he acted like he knew Lilia. But if Aunt Sandra is telling the truth, she hasn't seen her in almost a year. Her relationships never last long. Seems weird to me."

"Yeah, he doesn't strike me as a nice guy." Dawson slanted a glance her way. "You never mentioned that you knew Cade Maddox?"

"I'd forgotten about him until Aunt Sandra mentioned his name. He came for dinner once at Nana Grace's. You weren't there for some reason, although I can't remember why. It was a disaster. He showed up high and got drunk as well. Lilia and I had a big fight about it." She bit her lip. It was possible she'd never mentioned the incident to Dawson on purpose. Too embarrassing. "Just another one of our arguments. By that point, I'd grown tired of talking about them."

"I never got tired of hearing about them."

"Why not? I sure did."

"Because it mattered to you." Something shifted in his expression. A flicker of vulnerability, there and gone. As if he'd said more than he intended. His jaw tightened and his gaze fixed firmly on the road ahead.

"You're a good man, Dawson." Peyton studied his profile as Dawson entered the freeway. The strong nose and masculine mouth. She'd missed him. A question had been nagging at her since she left the hospital, and she couldn't hold it back any longer. "Can I ask you something personal?"

He arched a brow in her direction. "Depends on the question."

She swallowed hard. "Are you... seeing anyone?"

His hands tightened on the steering wheel. "No."

Relief flickered through her, unwelcome and undeniable. She tamped it down. "I'm surprised." Peyton kept her tone light and teasing. "There can't be that many eligible bachelors in Knoxville."

His mouth quirked, but it didn't quite reach his eyes. "You'd be surprised." Dawson was quiet for a long moment. "What about you?"

"No." The word came out softer than she intended. "I haven't... there hasn't been anyone. Not since."

He released a breath, and Peyton nearly swore she saw relief crease his features, but then he deliberately straightened his shoulders, as if physically reinforcing whatever internal walls were threatening to crumble. The quiet that followed felt loaded, like they were treading too close to forbidden territory. There was so much Peyton wanted to say, so much she wanted to explain, but Dawson's rigid posture stopped her. He'd asked her to table the discussion until the case was over. She needed to respect that request.

Peyton turned toward the windshield and put the conversation back in neutral territory. "Where to now?"

"The police station. Chief Garcia is putting together a task force, and he invited us to join them. We can update everyone on what we learned from Sandra."

"Sounds good." Peyton glanced at the sideview mirror. She stiffened. "Dawson… we may have a problem. White van, three cars back. He's driving like a maniac."

As if he was trying to catch up to them. Even as she turned around to look out the back window, the van swerved past a sedan and sped up. The driver's side window rolled down, and instantly, she knew what was about to happen.

"Gun!"

NINE

Dawson's stomach dropped, and he hit the gas just as a spray of bullets slammed into his SUV. He instinctively ducked low. Glass shattered. Frigid air rushed in, icing his fingers. Time seemed to slow as his brain assessed everything in a fraction of a second. Peyton, crouched low in the passenger seat. A box-store truck lumbering in the slow lane in front of them, and a family-sized sedan half a mile ahead. He imagined a mom and kids, just returning home from school or on their way to soccer practice.

Innocent civilians.

The van surged closer.

"Hold on!" Dawson jerked the wheel to the left, cutting across a lane. A horn blared. The white van with the business logo on the side slowed slightly before swinging into their lane, filling the rearview mirror. Two figures were visible inside. The barrel of an assault rifle emerged from the open passenger-side window. Dawson weaved in the lane in a desperate attempt to make them harder to hit. "Stay down!"

Bullets thunked against the metal. Something whispered past his head a second before the windshield splintered, creating a spiderweb that made visibility difficult. Dawson continued to swerve within his lane. His attention was split between the van and the other vehicles on the road. The last thing he wanted was to endanger more people by causing an accident, but he feared it might be impossible to prevent one.

God, I need Your help. The prayer was automatic and instinctive. Dawson was wise enough to know there was only so much within his control. *Protect us and the others on the road with us.*

The second the bullets stopped, Peyton popped out of her crouch, gun in hand. She twisted in her seat and returned fire.

The van backed off.

"Good work." Dawson wasted no time grabbing his radio. He pressed the button and started firing off information only to belatedly realize the instrument had been damaged in the gunfire. He tossed the handset down. The van surged forward again. "Peyton, call dispatch."

Dawson couldn't drive at these reckless speeds while fishing his cell phone from his pocket. Peyton swiveled in her seat again, fired off a couple of rounds, and then ducked low. Seconds later, she was shouting to be heard over the wind tunnel created by the shattered windows. Dawson cut into the next lane to avoid a slow-moving Lincoln. He weaved and bobbed through traffic, trying desperately to keep a distance between them and the white van. But the assailants dogged them.

He had to lose them. Before someone ended up dead.

Slipping into the far-left lane, he made a desperate plan. "Peyton, hold on." Gritting his teeth, he surged forward, increasing his speed far beyond the limit. Three lanes of traffic. His brain calculated the distance between vehicles in the other lane. As the exit sign loomed large, at the last second, he jerked his wheel across multiple lanes of traffic and sailed down the ramp to the feeder.

The van raced past them, overshooting the exit.

Dawson breathed a small sigh of relief. Sirens wailed in the distance. Backup was on the way. He hoped they'd be able to intercept the van, but he wouldn't take any chances. He barely tapped the brakes as he turned onto the road leading into town.

Peyton grabbed the dash. Her hair flew around her face. "Where are we going? They're getting away."

"My priority is protecting you." Dawson gripped the steering wheel, unwilling to even consider how close he'd just come to losing her. "You hurt?"

"No."

He sailed through a yellow light and spun into the parking lot of the Knoxville Police Department before circling to the rear of the squat red-brick building. Jax, gun in hand, waited at the door. Dawson slammed on the brakes, shoved the vehicle into Park, and bolted out of the driver's seat. By the time he'd crossed to Peyton's side, his buddy already had her out of the vehicle and was hustling her toward the safety of the building.

Dawson followed, casting a last glance at his vehicle. It was destroyed. Busted windows, dented metal. The attack couldn't have lasted over two minutes, but there was no doubt they'd barely escaped with their lives. "Thank you, God."

He let the door slam shut behind him. The sounds of voices and phones ringing echoed down the hall from the bullpen. News of the shooting would spread quickly. Dawson hurried to the nearest conference room. Peyton emerged just as he reached it, bumping straight into him, worry etched on her features. "Call your parents to check on Grace. Make sure she's okay."

"I've already sent an officer to the house," Jax added. "But he hasn't arrived yet."

The baby! How could he have forgotten about her! Dawson dialed his father's cell. Raymond answered on the first ring and assured him Grace was fine, currently nestled in his arms. Dawson shared the information with Peyton, and she sagged against the closest chair. Still on the phone with his father, he moved forward automatically and guided her into the seat. "There's been an incident. Peyton and I are okay, but I need you to stick close to Mom and Grace. An officer is en route to the house."

"Understood." Raymond didn't bother with questions. "Don't worry, son. I'll keep them safe."

"Thanks, Dad."

"Love you, son."

"Love you too."

He hung up, relief washing over him. Jax clapped

him on the back in a silent gesture of solidarity. "I'll get some waters and a first aid kit. Be right back."

Dawson nodded and then turned his attention to Peyton. Her hair was a wild mess, glass glinting from within the strands. She'd lowered her arms to the table and rested her forehead on them. Her shoulders sagged. A cut drew a line across the skin of her wrist, and even from his standing position, her body was visibly shaking. Worry cramped his insides. He placed a hand on her shoulder. "Peyton..."

"It's the adrenaline." She sucked in a shaking breath. "I was in a car accident a couple of years ago."

His chest tightened. Peyton wouldn't be this shaken up if it'd been a minor fender bender. Images of car accidents he'd responded to over the years hit him all at once. "How bad?"

"Bad."

The words came out in a whisper. Dawson's heart clenched, and he didn't think. He tugged her into a standing position and then into his arms. She was stiff for half a second, and then she relaxed into him, wrapping her arms around his waist. He lowered his cheek to her tangled hair. Nothing in this world felt more right than when Peyton was in his arms.

Memories came without warning. Stolen kisses and moonlight strolls. Running through the parking lot during a spring thunderstorm, Peyton laughing, her hair stuck to her face. Her lopsided grin when he caught her shaking her Christmas presents. The way she held his hand at his grandfather's funeral. Thousands of tiny, inconsequential moments that made up the fabric of his life.

It would be so much easier if he could stay angry with her. Keep her at arm's length. Goodness knows, he had good reason to. But that was like asking him to stop breathing—impossible, involuntary, pointless to try. Peyton was a part of him, no matter how much, at times, he wished otherwise.

The plan had been so simple. Protect her and Grace, solve the case, clear the air, and say goodbye. But he could feel it crumbling like sand beneath him. He'd been a fool to think this would ever be simple. His heart remembered what his mind had forced him to forget.

For fifteen years, he'd loved her. Completely. Utterly.

When she raised her head from his chest, and their eyes met, it felt like the most natural thing in the world to cup her face. Her skin was silky smooth under the pads of his fingers. He traced the curve of her cheek, as he had so many times before. Her breath caught. Those gorgeous lips parted, and her hazel eyes darkened with a familiar desire.

Every part of him ached to close that distance. To press his lips to hers and pretend the last five years hadn't happened. But they had. And a kiss in a conference room after a near-death experience wouldn't fix what was broken between them.

And things were broken between them, no matter what his heart said.

They were shattered. Irreparable.

Dawson released her and stepped back. The chair

behind him rolled across the room and slammed into the wall. He winced at the noise. The scent of jasmine clung to him, and his hands ached to hold her again. He needed to get out of this room. "I should update the chief on what happened. Check if they caught the van."

Peyton blinked, as if coming out of a haze. Her cheeks heated and her gaze skittered away from him. "Right. Yeah."

Dawson turned on his heel and crossed to the door. He resisted the urge to look back. He didn't want to know if he'd see regret or heartache on her face. What good would it do? There was only one way this ended, and it wasn't with them together.

He needed to keep his head in the game. Now more than ever. Solving this case wasn't just about Lilia and Grace anymore. Peyton's life was on the line too. Dawson would do whatever was necessary to protect her. And when it was all over, he would say goodbye.

He had to. There was no other choice.

TEN

Half an hour later, Peyton could still feel the heat of Dawson's hand cupping her cheek. She'd purposefully chosen a chair across the room from him, members of the task force filling the space between them, and yet it still didn't feel far enough. She'd almost kissed him. Been a breath away from it.

She'd dodged a bullet, in more ways than one.

Dawson was still angry. Peyton knew he cared for her —and probably always would—but she'd be foolish to think that was enough to erase the pain she'd caused by walking out the door. She'd hurt him. Deeply. Yes, she'd been a mess at the time, grieving and heartbroken, and so angry with herself and God and the world that none of Dawson's love could cut through. An explanation she prayed would blunt his pain once it was shared. But nothing she said would ever lead to him trusting her again.

They'd made vows. She'd broken them.

So yes, kissing Dawson would've been a terrible mistake. It would've only further entangled her heart and tipped the scales on what was already a delicate balancing act. They had a case to work together. Lilia's life was at risk, and Grace was in danger. Peyton needed to shove these feelings for Dawson into a vault and leave them there for the moment.

And when this was over... the best she could hope for was to part on good terms.

"Officers responded to the shooting, but the van disappeared before they could arrest the perpetrators." Chief Garcia sounded perturbed, and a deep frown creased his features. "I've put a BOLO out, but I'm not holding my breath. The license plate number Dawson provided belongs to a 2010 Nissan Frontier. Obviously stolen. A search for the name of the flower shop on the side of the vehicle yielded a chain of stores in Minnesota. The business has no connection to Texas or Knoxville. The perpetrators are probably using some kind of metal decal, one they can add and remove easily."

"Sounds organized." Liam's expression darkened. He was draped over the chair like he didn't have a care in the world, but his steely-eyed gaze belied that notion. "The Iron Serpents use stolen vehicles to move drugs and guns. Then they ship those vehicles south of the border to chop shops. We should check for reports of stolen white vans."

"It looked like a Ford." Dawson tapped his pen against the pad of paper in front of him. "Late 2000's model. Maybe older. It's probably worth checking for stolen vans, but if that's the case, why would they go to all the trouble to swap the plates? I bet this is a vehicle they use regularly."

"Either way the assault was planned." Jax gripped the back of a chair and leaned forward. "How did they know where you and Peyton were? Did they follow you from the ranch?"

"Doubtful. I was keeping watch."

"Bobby, my aunt's boyfriend, could've called someone. Tipped them off." Peyton felt Dawson's eyes on her, and she purposefully avoided looking in his direction. Instead she focused on the chief. "Was anyone able to figure out who Bobby is?"

"I did." Detective Noah Hodge stood. He removed a photograph from a manila folder before attaching it to the whiteboard at the front of the room with a magnet. "Meet Robert Paulson. Career criminal. His rap sheet includes domestic violence, second-degree assault, drug charges, and robbery. He's currently on parole for a drug conviction from sixteen months ago. Lists Sandra Morrison's house as his residence."

"How long has he lived there?"

"A year."

Peyton tilted her head. "According to my aunt, the last time she saw Lilia was last winter, so there's a chance Bobby and Lilia crossed paths then. Does Bobby have any connection to the Iron Serpents?"

"Don't know yet. I'm still digging into that. His parole guidelines forbid him from associating with criminals, but we all know how that goes. If Bobby is involved with the biker gang, it's in his best interest to keep that on the down low."

"Could explain why he was so upset to find two police officers in his house," Dawson said. "What about the guy who attacked Peyton at the hotel? Marvis Harrison."

"He's vanished." Liam scowled. "I tracked down a girlfriend of his. She confirmed he's a member of the Iron Serpents."

"We just keep coming back to them." Peyton ran down everything she'd learned from the visit with her aunt, including the fact that Lilia was dating Cade Maddox. "She told Aunt Sandra that she was going away for a while. No explanation why. That was last winter, probably about a year ago. Maybe less. So maybe Cade is Grace's father."

Stunned silence followed the statement.

She glanced around at the shocked faces in the room, her gaze finally landing on Dawson. Peyton arched her brows, her tone pointed. "Care to tell me what I'm missing?"

He grimaced. "Cade is the leader of the Iron Serpents."

Peyton's mouth dropped open. "You're kidding?" It was hard to imagine that the stoner she'd met while on spring break was now the leader of an organized criminal operation. "Aunt Sandra described him as a good-time guy, someone who wouldn't care about a kid he sired. Why on earth would he try to kidnap Grace? Or shoot at me? It would only bring attention to him and the Iron Serpents."

"Those are good questions." The chief steepled his fingers. "Ones we can't answer yet. Let's go over what we know, focusing on the facts, and starting with the night Lilia disappeared. Peyton, please start us off."

"Lilia calls me around seven in the evening, and says she's in trouble and needs my help. She promises to explain everything in person and asks me to come to the abandoned train depot at nine the same night. When I arrived, neither Lilia nor her car was there. I called Dawson for backup, and then heard a woman scream. I entered the train depot to investigate and provide aid, and was attacked by an unknown individual. He disarmed me with a knock to the head, and then attempted to shoot me, but because of our struggle, the shot went wide. I disarmed him and became embroiled in hand-to-hand combat."

"When I arrived on the scene," Dawson picked up where she left off, "I noticed Peyton's truck in the parking lot and heard gunshots. I found Peyton involved in a physical altercation with one perpetrator, but before I could assist, was shot at by another perpetrator. I returned fire and both men escaped into the woods. Afterward, Peyton and I discovered Grace hidden inside an empty railcar."

"A handgun was recovered from the scene—a Ruger SR9." Jax rose and added a photograph of the weapon to the whiteboard. "We believe this is the weapon the perpetrator attempted to shoot Peyton with. Forensics couldn't recover fingerprints from the gun. Bullets collected from the scene were run through the national database, but there were no matches to any other previous crimes." He paused. "This isn't a fact, but based on my experience, the weapon looked brand-new."

"Makes sense if we think the Iron Serpents are involved. A bandana with their logo was found at the crime scene." Noah removed his cowboy hat and tossed it on the table before running a hand through his hair. The strands stuck up in odd patterns. "The Iron Serpents traffic in illegal guns. Probably safe to assume the perpetrator that shot at Dawson was also using a new weapon. It's common for experienced criminals to do so in order to cover their tracks."

Chief Garcia nodded. "Can we prove Lilia was actually at the train depot? How do we know that the person Peyton heard screaming wasn't someone else?"

"I can help with that." Texas Ranger Felicity Capshaw raised a hand. The modest diamond wedding set on her left hand winked in the fluorescent lights.

Before the meeting began, as everyone was introduced to Peyton, she learned that Felicity and Noah were childhood friends who'd fallen in love while working a case. Even if she hadn't been told, the loving looks they shared when they thought no one was looking would've given it away.

"A blood pool at the scene near the west side of the railcar indicated there was an altercation." Felicity shot Peyton a sympathetic look. "It wasn't enough to suggest someone had died, but the person was injured. I asked the lab to put a rush on the DNA. Full confirmation will take a few more weeks, but we submitted a cheek swab from baby Grace for a familial comparison. Results came back this morning. The blood at the scene is a parent-child match to Grace. I think it's safe to assume Lilia was there."

Peyton had already known that, but knowing there was evidence to prove it still impacted her. Lilia had been bleeding. Hurt. There was no way to know how badly. Silence filled the room, as if everyone was echoing her same fears.

Lilia might already be dead.

A sour taste filled her mouth, and Peyton grabbed the water bottle in front of her. The cool liquid trailed down her throat but did little to ease her roiling emotions. She shoved them back and wiped her lips with the back of her hand, forcing her brain to think logically. "How did Lilia get there? To the train depot? Grace was in a car seat when we found her, and it makes sense Lilia would have to drive there, but her car wasn't found at the scene."

"Correct." Liam reached into his pocket and pulled out a tin of peppermints. He opened it and silently offered one to Peyton. "She has a 1999 Toyota Camry registered to her name, and we found evidence that a car was parked on the road south of the train depot based on a fresh oil stain. A BOLO's been issued for the vehicle, but so far, we haven't had any hits."

"We also don't know where she's been living for the last year," Jax added. "Lilia's last known address is in Austin. Travis County deputies went there and discovered that Lilia moved out a little over a year ago. No forwarding address."

"What about bank accounts?" Peyton asked, shifting the peppermint to the side of her cheek so she could talk better. "Credit cards? She had to be paying her bills somehow."

"Her bank account has about ten bucks in it and hasn't been touched since moving out of her old apartment. She doesn't have any credit cards, as far as I can tell."

Frustration bit at her. "What about the number she called me from?"

"Burner phone," Felicity piped in. "It was bought last month from a shop in Austin. I contacted them for surveillance video, but the system records over itself after a week. Even Grace's birth certificate lists her old Austin address, and the clinic Lilia gave birth at specializes in helping low-income women and families."

"So Lilia moves out of her apartment about a year ago, and then what? Drops off the face of the planet except for when she gave birth to Grace?" Peyton's brows drew together. "Doesn't that strike anyone else as weird?"

"Definitely. But it's possible she was living with someone. A boyfriend, maybe. Which brings us back to Cade Maddox." Felicity's expression grew speculative. "Lilia and Cade had dated before, as teenagers. Those kinds of relationships can stick. What if Lilia moved in with him, got pregnant, but then left before having Grace. Cade is a violent guy. I could see her being afraid of him."

Peyton nodded. She could easily envision that too. "She goes into hiding. Gives birth to Grace, but doesn't put Cade on the birth certificate. She's worried something will happen to her, so she draws up guardianship papers. And then... what? She called me in a panic."

"Cade found her." Dawson's expression darkened. "If Lilia left him, he'd be furious. Cade isn't the kind to let it go."

Jax's face screwed up in disbelief. "Guys, I can see Cade hurting Lilia, but kidnapping Grace? Why? He's never struck me as the kind of guy who'd want to change diapers or handle school drop-offs."

"I would normally agree with you," Felicity said, casting a knowing glance toward Noah. "But his relationship with Lilia might be different. More... powerful. Grace may be someone he cares about very much, and there's no way he'd ever gain custody of her legally. He'd have to take her. That could also explain why Peyton and Dawson were shot at today. Peyton is Grace's guardian. With her out of the way, it makes nabbing Grace a lot easier."

It was a good theory. One worth pursuing. Peyton planted her elbows on the table. "We need to interview him."

"Cade Maddox isn't going to willingly talk to any of us." Jax waved a finger around the room. "He's smart enough to lawyer up immediately. And he's not on parole, so we have no reason to drag him in."

"He might talk to me." Peyton absently ran a finger over the fresh cut on her hand. "Lilia is my cousin, and

I met Cade once. It could be enough to lower his guard."

"You kicked Cade out of your house," Dawson argued. A deep scowl darkened his features, and his tone was hard. He definitely didn't like this idea. "I doubt he remembers the interaction fondly."

"All the more reason for me to go. He was a braggart even back then. Cade'll be thrilled to one-up me now."

"Absolutely not. It's too dangerous."

She rolled her eyes. "I appreciate the concern, Dawson, but I'm perfectly capable of handling myself with criminals. I've been doing it for years."

Liam tilted his head. "Hate to break it to you, Dawson, but she has a point."

That earned him a glare from Dawson.

Peyton turned to face Chief Garcia. "I know Lilia is my cousin, and that makes this case personal, but I'm requesting to officially join the task force. The interview with my aunt proves I can be an asset, and I promise to follow orders. I have no interest in risking my badge, but I would like the opportunity to help in any way I can."

Chief Garcia assessed her for a long moment. His expression was inscrutable.

She held her breath. If he said no, there was nothing Peyton could do about it. She forced herself to meet his iron gaze dead-on. Her insides quivered with nerves. She'd faced down hardened criminals and had worked with some of the toughest law enforcement officers in the country, but all of them could take a lesson from Chief Sam Garcia.

Then his expression softened. "Special Agent Hughes, welcome to the team."

The knot in her chest loosened as she gave him a sharp nod. "Thank you, sir." Peyton surveyed the room, noting Dawson's resigned expression. He'd lost the battle, but she knew he'd insist on coming with her to interview Cade. She wouldn't fight him on it. Peyton was daring, but she wasn't a fool. Walking into a biker bar without backup would be reckless. "Let's make a plan for my interview with Cade."

ELEVEN

The home base of the Iron Serpents was Sidewinders, a bar positioned close enough to the highway for easy escape, but hidden from view behind a wall of trees. The dirt parking lot was packed with expensive motorcycles, chrome glinting in the faint moonlight. A few trucks were scattered near the back, and a lone sedan that looked completely out of place. Voices from a group of men dressed in leather vests carried across the distance. Dawson felt their eyes track his SUV. He had the sense, even in the darkness and the borrowed vehicle, they'd been made as law enforcement.

No one came to Sidewinders uninvited, except cops.

Peyton leaned closer to the windshield, presumably to get a better look at the bar. The low, flat-roofed structure was dimly lit, the blacked-out windows sufficiently hiding whatever was going on inside. "How would anyone know this is a bar? It doesn't even have a sign."

"That's by design." Dawson killed the engine. "Cade

pretends it's his only source of income, but it's actually used to launder funds gained from illegal sources. The only people who visit Sidewinders are members of the Iron Serpents, their families, and a few old, loyal friends of Larry's."

"Larry?"

"He ran the biker gang until his death a year and a half ago. That's when Cade took over. He was Larry's top lieutenant. Learned everything the old man knew and proved he had the brains and the ruthlessness to keep the operation running."

Peyton hummed, flipping down the visor to apply a fresh coat of gloss to her lips. "Surprising. The Cade I knew was headed nowhere fast. Not that being in charge of a criminal enterprise is a step in the right direction, but you get my drift."

"These guys believe they have a brotherhood, and will do whatever is necessary to protect their leader. Cade is careful to promote the most loyal members among his crew, and so far, it's paid off. We've tried over and over again to get someone to turn on him. Last year, one of his top guys was charged with murder. A robbery that went wrong. We offered manslaughter if he'd inform on Cade. He flat-out refused. Was convicted of first-degree murder and went away for life without parole." Dawson turned to face Peyton. "Don't underestimate the snake pit you're about to enter. These guys could shoot us, and all of them would lie about what happened. They'll say whatever they're told."

She fluffed her hair before offering him a hard smile

and flipping closed the visor mirror. "I'll do my best not to irritate them then."

Before he could say anything else, she exited the SUV, her long legs eating up the distance to the bar. Dawson scrambled after her. She'd forgone her thick winter coat for a pair of hip-hugging jeans and a maroon sweater. Boots kept her feet warm and hid her ankle holster. With her hair long and loose down her back, she cut quite an image. If Dawson's adrenaline hadn't already started pumping, Peyton would've sent his heart into high gear. As it was, he wanted to toss her over his shoulder and haul her out of here.

Especially when the biker guarding the front door gave her an appreciative once-over.

"Looks like you're lost, sweetheart."

"Nope." Peyton drew to a stop in front of him. "I'm here to see Cade Maddox."

He crossed his arms over a meaty chest. "Then you wasted your time because he's not here."

The hair on Dawson's arms rose as he clocked movement along the side of the building. They'd attracted attention from the group smoking outside. Some of them stamped out their cigarettes and moved closer, as if anticipating a fight. Several were visibly armed.

"Tell him Peyton Hughes is here to see him." Her tone was full of confidence, and her smile bordered on smug. "Trust me, he's gonna want to speak to me." Peyton tossed a lazy wave toward the group closing in. "Hey, boys. No need to get your boxer shorts in a knot. We're not here to cause trouble."

The guard at the door jerked his thumb toward one of the guys. "Ricky, get in there and tell Cade this woman is here to see him."

Ricky broke away from the crowd. He was bald with a tattoo snaking up the right side of his neck, and the confident swagger of a man in his element. Nothing about him stood out, and yet he pinged Dawson's internal warning system. Before he could place why, Ricky disappeared inside the bar. He emerged a moment later to give Peyton an assessing look. "Boss says she can come in."

"Told ya." Peyton lifted her chin as Ricky let her pass.

When Dawson attempted to follow, he was met with two walls of flesh as the guard at the door and Ricky blocked his entrance. Momentary panic hit him. He couldn't let Peyton go in there alone, but fighting would likely get him killed. He started running through possible strategies when static erupted from the guard's walkie-talkie, and a voice filtered out. "Let the husband in too."

The guard and Ricky stepped aside without a word.

Dawson followed Peyton inside.

The bar stank of cigarette smoke, beer, and body odor. A long bar took up most of one wall. Mismatched tables and chairs were scattered across a scratched plank floor covered in peanut shells. Country music spilled from a dented jukebox. The crowd was mostly bikers playing pool and darts. An assortment of women draped over barstools or the man of their choice.

And along the back wall, just past the dance floor, sitting on an elevated stage with a full view of the room was Cade.

His dark eyes locked onto her. Like a predator that had just found its prey. Peyton swallowed the urge to run and let her hips sway a little as she crossed to him. Dawson followed close behind. His steady presence gave her the confidence to keep her attention on Cade.

Dawson had her back. He wouldn't let anyone hurt her.

"Well, well, well, if it isn't Princess Peyton." Cade's gaze swept over her body from the top of her head down to her feet and then back up, lingering a bit on her chest before drifting back to her face. "I never thought you looked much like Lilia, but after all this time, I can see the family resemblance."

The nickname gave her a jolt. It was the same one Sandra always used. A coincidence? Could be. Cade had dated Lilia years ago, and her aunt had called Peyton that for as long as she could remember.

Surrounding Cade like a group of courtiers were bikers sporting enough ink and piercings to keep the only tattoo parlor in Knoxville busy for years. Peyton reached for a chair one of the men was leaning on and flipped it around before straddling it. She'd interrupted their poker game. Picking up the cards on the table, she frowned. "Ouch. Pair of twos. Someone should thank me for distracting you, Cade."

A low laugh escaped him, and his expression softened, even if his gaze didn't lose that predatory look. Peyton understood it. What her cousin had seen in him. Chiseled features, jet-black hair, and muscles for days. Unlike his comrades, he only had a few visible tats. Coupled with his arrogance and a charm he could turn on and off at will, he had bad-boy written all over him. For a woman desperate for male attention, Lilia wouldn't have stood a chance.

Peyton dropped the cards. Time to get to the point. "I suppose you've heard. Lilia's missing."

"I did." Cade's attention flickered toward Dawson before focusing back on Peyton. It was the first time, other than allowing him into the bar, that Cade had paid her ex-husband any mind. "I figured you're here cuz you think I had something to do with it. For efficiency's sake, it's better to clear the air. I haven't seen Lilia in over a year."

"But you were dating her?"

"For a while." He leered. "I'm thinking I chased the wrong cousin."

Peyton smothered the shudder of revulsion rippling down her spine. She began collecting the cards from the table and stacking them. "So the baby isn't yours then?"

Cade didn't miss a beat. "No."

"Funny, she looks a bit like you."

That earned her a laugh. "Next thing you know, you'll be asking for my DNA."

"Well..." She gave him a predatory smile of her own.

"If you're offering, I won't say no. It's a good way to put this to rest once and for all."

Cade picked up a glass of beer from the table. He drained it, licked the rim with deliberate slowness, and then handed the glass to Dawson. "Here."

Peyton blinked in surprise. She didn't know whether to be happy or disappointed at the prospect that Grace wasn't Cade's daughter.

Happy. Definitely happy.

As soon as Dawson took the glass, Cade's hand shot out and grabbed Peyton's arm. He pulled her into a standing position. Dawson lunged, but two of Cade's men caught him. The glass in his hand tumbled to the floor in the struggle and shattered into pieces. Peyton stared at the shards.

Cade completely ignored the commotion between Dawson and his men. "This is one of my favorite songs." His voice was smooth as honey. "Dance with me, Princess Peyton."

She nodded automatically, and as he turned to lead her onto the dance floor, Peyton shot Dawson a reassuring glance. His expression was thunderous, but the men holding onto him loosened their grip. He made no move to follow her. Peyton appreciated the way he let her call the shots. He didn't like it—she knew that much—but he respected her enough professionally to do things her way.

Cade wrapped an arm around her waist, cupping her other hand within his meaty one. He pulled her close. Peyton's insides revolted at the touch, but she leaned into it all the same, letting him take control of the dance. He swayed her along to the sound of the country music ballad. "Your husband looks irritated." His tone was amused.

"Ex-husband," she corrected. She wanted to create as much distance between her and Dawson as possible. Cade had basically ignored him, but he'd allowed Dawson into the bar for a reason, and she sensed the undercurrent of male hostility. "He'll get over it."

"I'm surprised he let you go."

"He didn't have a choice."

"And yet... here you are... in my bar. Together."

"He's helping me find Lilia." She pulled back far enough to look him in the face. "That's all I want, you know. To find my cousin. The rest doesn't matter as long as she comes home alive."

Cade hummed, forcing them back together again. His breath was hot against her ear. "You're walking a dangerous line, Princess Peyton. I happened to like Lilia, which is why I'm cooperating, but this is a one-time deal. I didn't have anything to do with her disappearance."

"What about the attempted kidnapping of her child?"

"Also not me." His hand slid up and down her back. "I gave you my DNA. I have nothing to hide."

"What you gave me is now shattered all over the floor."

He shrugged. "It's not my fault your ex bungled things."

"They knocked it out of his hand. Don't insult my intelligence, Cade."

His hand tightened on hers. "Don't insult mine. I don't care about Lilia's rugrat, and I'm not foolish enough to target two cops."

"Then members of your group did. We have evidence."

"My men don't blink without permission."

"Well, then we have a problem."

"Do we?" Cade's tone was once again amused, but when he leaned back to look her in the face, there was none of it in his expression. It was cold. Hard. Deadly. "I'll say it again, Princess Peyton, you're walking a dangerous line. If I were you, I'd focus my attention somewhere else. It'd be a shame if something happened to you or your *ex*-husband."

The threat chilled her blood. Still, Peyton kept her expression schooled and her tone even. "If you didn't have anything to do with Lilia's disappearance, then someone is working hard to make it look like you did. Isn't that a problem?"

"For me. Not you." He touched her nose, a silent warning to keep it out of his business. Then his mouth quirked. "Turnabout is fair play. Get out, Princess Peyton. And take your pet with you."

Cade suddenly released her, catching her off-guard. She stumbled, and laughter spread around the room. A second later, Dawson was at her side. He caught her elbow and hurried her toward the exit.

The echo of Cade's laughter followed her into the parking lot.

TWELVE

Dawson picked up another hay bale and tossed it from the back of the truck onto the stacked pile in the barn. Sweat beaded on his brow. He'd shed his jacket and sweater a while ago, the frigid air a welcome relief. It'd been a full day since they'd left Sidewinders, but not even physical labor had improved his mood. Every time he thought about Cade touching Peyton, rage rolled through him again.

It was an anger he had no right to. He knew that. Peyton had done her job and done it well.

But it was there all the same.

The barn door hinges creaked, and he sensed her before she spoke. Dawson stiffened. He bent down and hefted another hay bale out of the old work truck. Then her voice reached him, floating across the space. "Where are all the horses?"

"In the new barns." His words were clipped. Cool as the wintry night. He chucked another bale.

"Is everything okay?" Peyton leaned casually against an empty stall. She looked beautiful and relaxed in a tracksuit, her hair tossed up into a casual ponytail. "You've been pretty quiet all day, since church this morning, and you ran out so fast after dinner that you missed dessert."

"I didn't want any." He could barely force himself to sit at the table and choke down the meal.

Her brows arched in disbelief. "Peach cobbler is your favorite."

Dawson didn't answer. There was nothing he could say that wouldn't start an argument, so he chucked another hay bale from the truck. It landed in place, and then toppled from the spot, landing in a heap on the floor. He'd thrown it with too much force.

"I was hoping we could talk about Cade and what happened last night."

"We already did." She'd told him what they'd discussed during the dance, when he was out of earshot. Thinking of it again spiked his heart rate. He tossed the last bale from the truck and ripped off his work gloves. The exertion had left his body weary, but his mind was still unsettled.

"Yeah, but I've been thinking, and I have some theories."

He didn't answer. He couldn't talk about Cade. Not yet. "We'll discuss it tomorrow."

Peyton frowned. "Are you angry with me?"

He jumped from the truck. "I'm tired, and I want to get this work done."

"Really? Cuz it seems like you're mad at me."

He was, but he also knew he couldn't talk about this without losing his temper. And it wasn't fair to Peyton. She was worried sick about Lilia, and while she was handling it well, he knew there was a breaking point. Dawson tossed his gloves through the open window of the truck.

Peyton threw up her hands in exasperation. "You always do this. You stew and grumble and avoid until I force you to face what you don't want to say. It's so frustrating! Just spit it out, Dawson. I don't need you to protect me."

"You don't need me to..." He sputtered. "Were you there last night? You waltzed into a biker bar and deliberately provoked the most dangerous man in the room. You put yourself in danger, and for what? We're no closer to figuring out where Lilia is. The only thing we accomplished was putting you on Cade's radar."

She planted her hands on her hips. "In case you haven't noticed, I was already on his radar. Or did the bullets in your truck yesterday afternoon not send a big enough message?"

"Those might not have been from Cade. We know the Iron Serpents are involved in some way, but it's not clear Cade is calling the shots. It could be someone challenging him for leadership and taking advantage of the situation." Dawson felt his voice rise. "What I know is that you've been warned. If you step wrong in this investigation, and Cade feels threatened, he will kill you. No questions asked."

The very thought made him sick and fueled his temper. He was angry at her for putting herself in harm's way, and more angry with himself for caring so much. "What are the chances I have of convincing you to step back and let us handle this investigation? None."

Frustrated with himself for yelling, he turned away from her and braced his hands on the empty horse stall. He felt rather than heard her move closer, then a hand came to rest on his back. "Dawson."

The softness in her voice urged him to speak the truth. "I hated it. Standing by and watching that criminal put his hands on you...I haven't felt that helpless since..." His voice choked up.

"Since Samuel died," she finished softly.

He shook his head, trying hard to dislodge the images crowding his mind. Her tear-stained cheeks, lying in bed in the dark, day after day, shuffling around the house in a robe, her face gaunt and haunted. "I couldn't protect you then either. I tried... God knows I tried."

"So do I." She ducked under his arm until they were face-to-face. "What happened to me after Samuel died wasn't your fault. I was lost, Dawson. In more ways than one. Nana Grace's death crushed me, losing our child... it felt like a punishment. Like God had turned his back on me. My faith disappeared. I was angry and so heartbroken that I couldn't see past my own grief. I felt alone."

"You weren't alone. I was there. Right there the whole time."

"I couldn't see that. I was angry with you for going

back to work, for having dinners with your family. You found solace in church and with your friends. And..."

"And what?" His voice didn't sound like his own. It was raw and barely above a whisper. "And what, Peyton? I didn't love him? Didn't feel the loss?"

"I didn't say that—"

"But it's what you meant." He turned away from her, his body heat rising. "I held it together. For you. Because you were shattered, and I couldn't bear to add my grief to yours. So I forced myself to put one foot in front of the other. I went back to work so we could pay the bills. I spent time with my family because it was the only place I felt I could breathe. And I went to church to pray for strength, to be the man you needed in order to get through a loss no one should have to bear."

The words were coming fast now, tumbling over themselves as if a cork had been popped on his feelings and he could no longer keep them in. "I thought once you were better, once you were past the worst of your grief, it would be my turn. That I could fall apart. Share my pain. But that never happened." Dawson looked at her, the hurt and the betrayal pouring out of him. "Because you left. I needed you. Needed my wife, and you... just left."

Tears spilled over her cheeks. Peyton let them fall unabated. "I didn't know."

"You didn't stick around long enough to find out."

She stiffened and wiped the tears from her cheeks. "That's not fair. You're right, I shouldn't have left, but you should've told me what you were feeling. You keep it all inside, Dawson, and never come to me. I've always had to nudge and urge and poke until you finally open up."

He couldn't believe this. "So it's my fault you left?"

"No, I take responsibility for my part, but a marriage takes two. I was shattered, you're right. I didn't have the emotional capacity to drag your feelings out of you the way I did before. You hid your grief so well, Dawson. I knew you were hurting. I knew you loved him. But..." She balled her hand into a fist and pounded her own chest. "I felt like someone had ripped out my heart. If I'd known you felt the same..."

He had. He had felt the same. "It would have changed things?"

"We'll never know." Peyton lowered her hand. "And it does neither of us any good to play what if. You said it before at the hospital. We both made mistakes. And I'm sorry, Dawson. Truly sorry."

He felt the anger seep from him. "I'm sorry too. I should've spoken up when Nana Grace died. You were hurting, and I thought that time and love would help you move past that grief, but then we lost Samuel, and it all fell apart."

Suddenly, all the anguish he'd swallowed down came rushing up. His body shook as tears filled his eyes. He sank down to the bale of hay and buried his face in his hands.

Peyton's arms encircled him. Soft. Tender. Loving. He reached for her, pulling her into his lap.

And sobbed. Cried for his son. For the life they

should've had. Dawson let it all out, in a way he'd never allowed himself to do. When it was over, he was spent. Peyton slid from his lap to the hay bale and rested her cheek on his shoulder. Her face was blotchy from crying too, her eyes swollen, but she held his hand in hers, not breaking the contact.

How long they stayed like that, Dawson couldn't have said. The silence was comforting, the sweet scent of the hay and the drift of nighttime sounds soothing. His mind wandered. Through those days after Nana Grace died, after Samuel passed. How he'd been scared and worried, but never said so out loud.

He'd tried to protect her. And in doing so, he might very well have pushed her further away.

Dawson didn't want to make the same mistake again. He ran his thumb over the back of her hand. "I'm scared for you, Peyton. And for Grace. The Iron Serpents are dangerous, and whether or not Cade is behind this, we've kicked up a hornet's nest by challenging him."

She sighed. "I know. You're right. But it was also the only way to convince him to talk to us." Peyton tilted her head to look up at him. "And you're not the only one who's worried and scared. Cade let you into the bar. He was playing with us. With you."

"Okay, so where does that leave us? Worried and scared. What's the point of talking about our feelings again?"

She laughed. Her smile was contagious, and he smiled too.

Peyton poked him in the stomach. "The point is so

we both don't feel alone in our worries. We have each other. And God." She leaned against his shoulder again. "He's watching over us, Dawson. And Lilia and Grace. Don't forget that."

She was right, of course, but it surprised him to hear her say it. Peyton had always been a believer, but fully trusting God... turning to Him in times of trouble... that hadn't been something she used to do.

"I've been thinking about my conversation with Cade. Replaying it over and over again. I don't think he knows where Lilia is."

Dawson wasn't so convinced. "He's an expert liar. And a master manipulator."

"I'm not suggesting he can be trusted. I believe he is Grace's father. Or at least, thinks he is. That stupid trick he pulled with the glass showed his hand. But I think we need to consider that someone within the Iron Serpents is framing him in order to gain control." Peyton frowned. "And I have the feeling there's something we're missing about all of this."

"Like what?"

"I don't know. Cade has an ego, and I could easily see him being furious that Lilia left him, but he's not stupid. It's reckless to kidnap a baby and shoot at two members of law enforcement. It brings more attention to his criminal activities, which is the last thing he seems to want. If he's after her, it's not just about control or being scorned. It's bigger than that."

Her reasoning was sound, but if there was something more to this case, they hadn't found any evidence of it yet. "Liam is working on tracking down where Lilia was living at the time she gave birth to Grace. Let's see what he comes up with and go from there. In the meantime, I think you're right. We should look to other people within the Iron Serpents who might use this opportunity to challenge Cade." Dawson stood and extended a hand to help Peyton up. "For now, let's go back to the house. I suddenly have a hankering for peach cobbler."

Peyton's hazel eyes twinkled with amusement. "Oooo, too bad. It's all gone."

He shot her a stern look. "Don't joke about peach cobbler."

"Who's joking?" She climbed into the old work truck so they could drive it back to the carport near the house. "We all had seconds. It was fantastic. You really missed out."

His hand shot out and tickled her. "Tell the truth!"

She shrieked with laughter and twisted away, but he had her cornered in the truck. She grabbed his hand in desperation, trying to catch her breath. "You win, you win! We hid some peach cobbler behind the leftover roast beef so your dad wouldn't find it."

"We?"

"Your mom and I." She grinned. "I never knew how sneaky Ellen could be. She had me distract him with the baby while she hid the dessert. It worked like a charm though."

"Peach cobbler is his favorite too. He'll eat the whole tin if Mom let him." Dawson fired up the truck, and they bounced over the field to the house. The night had gone clear and cold, every star sharp overhead, but it was the warm lights glowing in the living room that held his attention. Home. He never tired of the sight. And somehow, it meant more to have Peyton in the truck beside him. Like a piece of his life that was missing had suddenly been snapped into place.

He circled the carport and pulled in. Peyton hopped out before he could open her door, meeting him at the back of the truck. He grabbed her hand, holding her in place before she could head toward the house. "Wait."

"What is it?"

The moonlight painted her face with an ethereal glow. The soft curve of her brow, the bow of her lip. Dawson didn't know how to explain what he was feeling. Only that he wanted one or two more stolen moments with her before entering the house. He wanted to hold on to this feeling between them.

A strand of hay was caught in her hair. Dawson stepped closer and detangled it.

Peyton's stilled. Her gaze searched his before landing on his mouth. There were a thousand reasons why this was a bad idea. The case, the danger, the five years of hurt between them. But standing here in the moonlight, with her looking at him like that, none of those reasons seemed to matter.

His hands found her face, tilting it up toward his. Her skin was cool from the night air, but silky soft. "I've missed you."

"I've missed you too."

He lowered his mouth to hers.

The kiss was soft at first. A brush of his lips against hers. Tentative. Tender. But then her arms wrapped around the back of his neck, pulling him closer, and the dam broke. Every ounce of longing he'd tried to bury since she burst back into his life broke free. He kissed her like he'd been starving for her. Because he had been. Every day. Every night. For five long years.

She was everything he'd lost but never stopped wanting.

When they finally broke apart, both of them were breathing hard. Peyton's hands slid down his neck to rest on his chest, but she didn't move out of the circle of his embrace.

"Dawson..." Her voice was barely a whisper.

"I know." He didn't know what came next. Didn't know if their relationship could be repaired. But right now, he couldn't bring himself to care. "That was... unwise."

"I'm not sorry though."

"Neither am I." He took her hand and started for the house. Then stopped mid-step halfway across the front lawn, as he finally registered the cold. "Hold on. I left my jacket in the truck."

Dawson jogged back to the vehicle and grabbed his coat. The hinges creaked as he slammed the door shut again. He patted the jacket pockets, searching for his cell phone. He was certain it—

"Dawson!" Peyton raced toward him, a look of terror on her face. Half a second later, her shoulder plowed into his midsection, taking him down hard. His body hit the unyielding ground, and the wind was knocked from him as she landed in a heap on top of him.

The crack of rifle fire split the night.

Bullets punched through the truck's rear panel, right where Dawson had been standing.

THIRTEEN

Peyton's heart thundered against her rib cage as she rolled off Dawson while reaching for her weapon. The grass was cold against her overheated skin, and the echo of Dawson's lips against hers felt like a distant memory, even though it'd only just happened. Her gaze scanned the yard, searching for the sniper. Moonlight trickled over the trees and the wide expanse of the driveway leading to the empty country road.

"Do you see him?" Dawson kept his voice pitched low. He was crouched beside her in the shadows of the carport, weapon in hand.

"No." Frustration colored her voice. "I'm not even sure where the shots came from."

Dawson reached for his dropped jacket and removed his cell phone from one of the pockets. He hit a button and a second later said, "Dad, we're okay, but stay inside. The ranch isn't secure." He paused and then whispered, "Understood."

He hung up and said, "Dad called 911. Backup is on the way."

That brought Peyton little comfort. "He was aiming for you." She kept her attention on the yard, hunting for movement. "He used a scope with a laser, so he may not even be on the property." Her attention was drawn to the house across the street. It was roughly 250 yards away, but still within striking range for a sniper with some experience. A decent hunter, with a good scope, could hit a human-sized target with little difficulty. "Your neighbors? The second-story window has a clear line of sight."

"Possibly."

Sirens wailed as patrol cars approached the ranch. Dawson and Peyton stayed where they were, in the shadows, until responding officers arrived. One of the patrol cars drove off the driveway into the grass and came to a stop, providing a shield between the carport and the house. Peyton recognized the driver. Officer Tucker Colburn. He'd been the first responding officer after the kidnapping attempt too.

Tucker opened the driver's side door, gun drawn. "I'm covering you."

Dawson rose, taking Peyton's hand. "Come on."

Staying low and using the patrol car as cover, they started for the safety of the house. With every step, Peyton expected shots to ring out. It was only after they crossed the threshold that the tension in her shoulders dropped.

Raymond came around the corner from the rear

bedroom, wearing his pajamas and holding a shotgun. Relief creased his features. "Praise God. Either of you hurt?"

"No." Dawson released Peyton's hand. "Mom and Grace?"

"Sheltering in the bathroom."

Dawson gave a sharp nod and then turned to Peyton. "Stay here. I'm going to help secure the property."

"No." She blocked him with her body. "The sniper was aiming for you. Going out there only endangers your officers. Give them time to clear the property and check the house next door."

His jaw tightened. "I'm not hiding in here like a coward."

"Then I'm going with you." Her tone brooked no argument. She was playing dirty but felt no regret about it. Dawson wasn't thinking clearly, and his stubbornness would get him killed. "Either we both go, or we both stay. Make your choice."

His cheeks heated with fury, and he didn't answer for a long moment. When he did, it was through gritted teeth. "Fine. I'll stay."

Dawson spun away from her, marching to the window near the door, and parted the curtain with one finger. He peeked out into the yard. Then he pulled his cell phone from his pocket. Based on his half of the conversation, he was speaking with Tucker.

Peyton trembled. She'd put on a brave front for Dawson because that's what was required to keep him in place, but terror settled into her like cold water. Why had the sniper gone for Dawson and not her? Was Cade sending a message?

Raymond joined her, a reassuring hand coming to rest on her shoulder. "Are you all right, darlin'?"

She pressed her lips together and shook her head. "I'm sorry. I've pulled danger straight to your family, and I'm so sorry for it."

"You have done nothing wrong, so don't you dare apologize." Raymond pulled her under the shelter of his fatherly embrace. "Ellen and I consider you family. You'll always have a place here with us."

His words brought a sting of tears to her eyes. The truth was, she wasn't their family anymore. She'd ruined all that when she divorced Dawson. Their passionate kiss outside might've revealed the truth—that they still cared deeply for one another—but it didn't erase the pain of their breakup. Could he ever trust her again?

Could they repair what they'd broken?

The swirling questions made her head hurt, and suddenly she felt exhausted. Or maybe it was the crash after the adrenaline rush. Either way, standing in the living room watching Dawson pace angrily in front of the windows wouldn't do one lick of good. She hugged Raymond and then said, "I'm going to check on Ellen and Grace."

She went down the hallway to the master bedroom. A handmade quilt covered the four-poster bed, and photographs of a marriage and a life with children lined the walls. It was cozy and sweet, and before her heart could ache too much, Peyton focused on the door leading to the bathroom. She knocked. "Ellen, it's Peyton. You can come out."

The lock clicked, and the door swung open. Ellen, wrapped in a soft robe, her hair in rollers, held Grace. The baby was awake, her happy babbling a stark contrast to the chaos happening outside. Peyton's heart melted at the sight. She reached for Grace, and when Ellen handed the baby over, cuddled her close. She sent up a prayer of thanksgiving. They were all safe. All okay.

She sank down onto the vanity seat. "Dawson and Raymond are in the living room, waiting for the patrol officers to clear the property. I think the sniper was across the street, at the Sutters' house."

Ellen seemed unfazed by the fact that a criminal had taken shots at one of her children. She tightened the belt on her robe. "I'd better put on a pot of coffee and start making sandwiches. It's gonna be a long night." She paused, brushing a hand over the top of Peyton's head in a comforting and motherly gesture. "I'm so glad you're okay, hon. The last few days have been a lot to take in. If you need to talk, or even just vent, I'm always available."

Her kindness tugged hard at Peyton's heart. For most of her life, Nana Grace had been her foundation. The one person she trusted without reservation. She'd had Dawson too—loved him fiercely—but a spouse differed from a family. Peyton had never fully let the Grahams become hers. She'd kept a careful distance, always aware that she'd married into their world but didn't quite belong to it. A girl from a broken home, raised by her grandmother, surrounded by a family so whole it sometimes made her feel lacking.

That decision had been a mistake. It'd left her isolated and alone after Nana Grace died. Not because the Grahams wouldn't have helped. She knew now they would have. In a heartbeat. But because Peyton had never given them permission to.

"I'm scared." She gently touched Grace's cheek. "I don't want anyone to get hurt, and it feels like there's no way to stop it. Lilia's still missing, and I'm terrified about what that means. Dawson and I..." She swallowed hard, not knowing if she was ready to talk about their kiss. "It's complicated. And on top of everything else, I'm the guardian of this beautiful baby girl, and what if... what if it's permanent? What will I do? Can I really raise her by myself? I could barely handle one night alone with her in a hotel room. And after Samuel..."

"Oh, hon." Ellen sat on the vanity bench next to her. "It probably doesn't feel this way, but you're actually doing an amazing job with Grace. When Dawson was first born, I nearly dropped him on his head."

Despite the seriousness of the situation, Peyton laughed. "No, you didn't."

"Hand to God. A nurse caught him, thank goodness, but taking care of a child is terrifying for everyone. I'd love to lie to you and say it gets easier, but honestly, it doesn't. But you learn. To trust yourself, to ask for help, and most importantly, to rely on God. Because our kids, they aren't really ours. They belong to Him. We just have them on loan."

Ellen again smoothed a hand over Peyton's hair. "Keep talking to the good Lord, hon. He's listening, and He will help you see your way ahead, even when everything feels scary and uncertain."

"I will." Peyton's faith was unwavering now, hard-won and rebuilt from the ashes of the darkest years of her life. She knew God was with her. Believed it with every ounce of her being. But knowing something in your heart and hearing it spoken aloud by someone who loved you were two different kinds of comfort.

She smiled at Ellen. "Thank you."

"Anytime, sweetie." Ellen gave her a sideways hug.

Peyton's cell phone rang, interrupting the tender moment. Grace, startled by the loud noise, jolted and then began crying. Ellen deftly took the baby so Peyton could quickly fish her phone out of her pocket. Unknown Caller flashed on the screen.

Lilia? Peyton's stomach lurched as she answered the call. "Hughes."

"I heard you've been looking for me. It needs to stop."

The rough male voice spilling from the speaker was unfamiliar. Peyton gripped her cell phone tighter. "Who is this?"

"The guy from the hotel."

Marvis. Peyton's blood chilled. She met Ellen's questioning gaze and mouthed, "Get Dawson." As Ellen hurried from the bathroom, Peyton focused back on the criminal. She put the call on speaker. "You've got a lot of nerve calling me after what you did. You tried to kidnap a child."

"I was under orders and didn't realize I was tangling with a cop. Look, I'm not the bad guy here. You've got bigger problems on your hands. Cade is going to kill you."

Peyton glanced up as Dawson appeared in the doorway. He clearly caught the last sentence in the exchange because his brows lifted. She scrambled for something to write on, and her gaze landed on a lipstick tube. She jotted Marvis on the mirror.

"Did you hear me?"

"Sorry, I'm in shock." She needed to keep Marvis talking. "Cade swears he has nothing to do with this."

"And you believe him? You're dumber than I thought."

"Why does he want to kill me?"

"Because he doesn't want you looking for Lilia. She stole something valuable from him, and Cade needs it to stay buried. He's working hard to cover his tracks, but things are falling apart quickly. There are people inside the Iron Serpents who are questioning his judgment and think he shouldn't be our leader anymore."

Suspicion prickled her. "Are you one of those people?"

"It don't matter whether I am or not. The point is you need to focus your attention on Cade and stay away from me. I'm not the bad guy here."

"Then come into the Knoxville Police Department and help us stop Cade."

He laughed bitterly. "Lady, he's got eyes and ears everywhere. I'll be dead before I hit a holding cell."

"We can protect you."

"You can't even protect yourself. Stop looking for Lilia. You won't find her."

"Wait!" Desperation pitched Peyton's voice higher as she sensed he was about to hang up. "What did Lilia steal from Cade?"

The only answer was dead air.

FOURTEEN

The next morning, Dawson stood in front of Chief Garcia. His boss was seated behind the broad expanse of his desk. Papers overflowed his plastic inbox, and on the credenza behind him were photographs of his family along with ones from various social events, including pictures with the mayor and city council. Smart and dedicated, the chief understood his job wasn't just about law enforcement but politics too. He balanced the two better than anyone Dawson had ever worked for.

"I've searched through everything we found at the train depot—Grace's car seat, the backpack, and the toys inside—but didn't find anything unusual," Dawson said. "If Lilia stole something valuable from Cade, she didn't hide it with the baby."

"Can we even be certain she stole anything?" Liam asked from his position on the other side of the room, where he leaned against a large bookcase. "When Marvis broke into the hotel room, he went for Grace. Why? If Cade's only interested in getting the evidence back, why steal the baby?"

"To use her as leverage." Peyton was seated in a visitor's chair, her posture was straight and her gaze unwavering. Ever the professional. But the dark circles shadowing the area under her eyes showed she hadn't slept any better than Dawson last night. "I don't think Cade knows where Lilia is. Or where she hid the evidence. He's trying to flush her out, and Grace is the way to do that."

Chief Garcia leaned forward. "And the attacks on you and Dawson?"

"Cade wants me to stop looking for Lilia. And I'm sure he's worried that I may stumble across whatever she stole." Peyton quickly glanced at Dawson before focusing back on the chief. "Last night was a message for me. The sniper used a scope with a red light, which he flashed over Dawson's body several times to attract my attention. He took the shot only after Dawson was on the ground. Cade wants me to know that if I don't stop looking for Lilia, he'll come after anyone I care about."

The chief looked at Dawson, his expression neutral. "Is that your assessment as well, Detective?"

"I agree it was a message, but I'm not sure Cade was the one who sent it. Jax reached out to a couple of his informants, and we've confirmed Marvis wants to take over the leadership of the Iron Serpents. He could be the one behind these attacks."

Peyton narrowed her gaze. "So now you believe Cade is being framed?"

"Oh, don't get me wrong, Cade doesn't want you meddling in his business, and he'll kill you in an instant if he feels threatened. But I don't trust Marvis either. He could be using this to his advantage, doing everything he can to put pressure on Cade and keep law enforcement breathing down his neck."

"True, but I agree it would be unwise to take anything Marvis says at face value." Chief Garcia frowned. "Where was the sniper?"

"Located across the street. My neighbors are in Florida visiting their daughter. The perpetrator broke into their home and used an upper-story window to gain a clear line of sight."

"Forensics worked their magic but didn't collect anything useful." Liam pushed away from the bookcase and claimed the other visitor's chair, hooking one arm over the back of the seat. "The perpetrator was also smart enough to collect his shell casings before fleeing, something that most newbie criminals forget in their panic to get away."

"So you think we're dealing with someone experienced?"

Liam shrugged. "At least moderately. But I don't agree with Peyton and Dawson. It's impossible to know why the sniper missed. It could've been a warning, designed to frighten Peyton, or the perpetrator could've gotten cold feet about shooting a law enforcement officer in cold blood. Either way, I don't think it matters. We should take precautionary measures."

Dawson opened his mouth to respond, but Peyton beat him to it. "Grace and I can move to a safe house. Our presence has put the Graham family in danger, and I don't want to risk that an innocent civilian will get hurt."

His gaze shot to her. Why hadn't she discussed this with him on the way to the police department this morning? Dawson knew her first priority was protecting Grace, and he believed Peyton wanted to protect his family, but a part of him wondered if this was a response to their kiss last night. A convenient excuse to put some distance between them.

They hadn't discussed what'd happened, or where they stood. Dawson wasn't even sure about his own feelings. He didn't regret kissing her, but one tender moment didn't erase the past. How could he reopen his heart to her when he didn't fully trust her to stay?

Even now, it felt like she was running. The thought wasn't entirely fair, and he knew it, but Dawson felt his own shields going up.

Peyton purposefully avoided looking at him, instead staying fixed on Chief Garcia. "I know your resources are limited, and finding Lilia has to be a top priority. With Grace and me hidden away, I hope you all can focus on solving the case."

"If the Knoxville PD had a safe house, I'd agree with you, but our budget doesn't allow for that."

"I can call my supervisor. Maybe he can swing something."

"I have a better idea." Chief Garcia rested his arms on his desk. "There's a group of former soldiers living in town. I've nicknamed them the Special Forces. They've assisted us with cases in the past, and when the occasion arises, they've provided protection details. We can ask them to guard the Graham property. This way, you can continue to assist on the case, but Grace and the ranch are protected."

"If I may, sir," Dawson interjected. "I've already arranged for the Special Forces to assist. Hayley and Tucker have created a schedule, and the first shift should arrive within the hour, allowing for the patrol officer currently stationed outside my house to return to his normal duties."

Officer Tucker Colburn and Assistant Chief Hayley Montgomery were both part of the Special Forces group. Tucker was a former Army Ranger, and Hayley worked as a military police officer before joining the Knoxville PD. After the sniper incident last night, they were some of Dawson's first phone calls.

Peyton turned to face Dawson. "You trust them? The Special Forces?"

"A hundred percent." He met her gaze. "Grace and my family will be safe. You don't need to worry."

Some of the tension in her shoulders eased. "Thank you."

"Good. Now that the matter is settled." Chief Garcia brought everyone's attention back to him. "Let's discuss where—"

A knock on the door interrupted him. Assistant Chief

Hayley Montgomery opened it and slipped inside. Her dark pixie cut was sharper than usual, and the sleeves of her button-down were rolled to the elbows, exposing the mottled scars on her right hand and the scripture tattoo on her inner wrist. At five months along, the slight swell of her belly was just visible beneath her shirt. "Sorry to interrupt, sir, but Supervisory Special Agent Derek Fallon from the ATF is here to see you. It's about the Lilia Morrison case."

Shock vibrated through Dawson. The ATF didn't make house calls to small-town police departments unless something big was at stake. He exchanged a look with Liam, who'd gone still in his chair.

Chief Garcia's expression didn't change, but his jaw tightened almost imperceptibly. "Send him in."

She nodded and then turned to Dawson. "I've scheduled the Special Forces to protect the ranch until the end of the week. If you need them longer than that, let me know, and we'll make arrangements."

He flashed her a grateful smile. "I appreciate it, Hayley."

She snorted, reaching for the door handle. "You may regret it once my husband arrives for tonight's shift. I'll send Walker with snacks, but he's been known to raid the fridge like a wild raccoon."

Dawson made a mental note to warn his mom. She'd be thrilled. The only thing that made her happier than taking care of babies and kids was feeding people.

Hayley left and returned moments later with a tall silver-haired man in an expensive charcoal suit. Chief

Garcia made the introductions, and SSA Derek Fallon politely shook everyone's hand before setting his briefcase on the corner of the desk. He declined Liam's offer to sit and positioned himself where he had a full view of the room.

"Forgive me for dropping by unannounced, but it's come to my attention that your missing person's investigation has run afoul of a federal investigation into the Iron Serpents and Cade Maddox. I'm not at liberty to discuss details, but we have assets in play. Your visit to Sidewinders drew attention and put my people at risk."

Dawson blinked in surprise. The ATF had undercover officers embedded in the Iron Serpents? Since when?

"We apologize, SSA Fallon, but we didn't know about a federal investigation into the Iron Serpents." Chief Garcia arched his brows. "It's customary for the local police department to be notified of such investigations in order to avoid an overlap that would put an undercover officer's life at risk."

Fallon acknowledged that with a slight nod. "There was a mix-up in our office."

The chief grunted. "And did you mistakenly forget to inform the Texas Rangers as well? Because they've been working with my department for months investigating the various aspects of the Iron Serpents' criminal enterprise."

"Casting blame at this point gets us nowhere, Chief. I'm here to handle the matter at hand. The ATF has been running an operation targeting the Iron Serpents, and we're close—closer than we've ever been—to dismantling the entire organization. We need your cooperation."

"What precisely are you asking for?"

"Stay away from Cade Maddox and the Iron Serpents."

Peyton opened her mouth, but Dawson placed a hand on her shoulder and squeezed. He knew Chief Garcia well and trusted him to handle this.

"SSA Fallon, I appreciate the delicate balance you need to strike, but what you're asking for is out of the question. We have direct evidence linking the Iron Serpents to Ms. Morrison's disappearance, and as it stands now, we believe she may be alive. I cannot stop pursuing leads or hold up our investigation. Not when a woman's life is at risk."

"Our intelligence suggests the Iron Serpents are not involved in your missing persons case."

Peyton inhaled sharply. "Is Lilia dead?"

Derek looked at her, and a flash of sympathy sparked before he buried it. "I don't know where your cousin is, Special Agent Hughes. What I do know is that my operation has eyes and ears inside the biker gang, and Lilia Morrison has not come up recently. If she were being held by the Serpents, we'd know it."

Dawson was tempted to ask what Fallon knew about the evidence Lilia supposedly stole, but he wasn't sure he'd get a straight answer. If the ATF undercover agents were embedded with the Iron Serpents and knew Lilia had taken evidence, then they should be looking for her too.

"Might I suggest a compromise," Chief Garcia said. "An ATF agent is welcome to join our task force. That way we can avoid stepping on your toes, but still have the freedom to pursue all leads."

"Chief, I don't think you understand. Pursuing the Iron Serpents in any way puts my people at risk and threatens an investigation we've spent nearly a year building. As fellow members of law enforcement, I would think that means something." His expression hardened. "I'm formally requesting your assistance in this matter, and hope you'll give it. I would hate for things to become political and messy."

Dawson rocked back on his heels. Who was this guy? He'd worked with federal agents before and found them to be cooperative and helpful. Fallon was making it clear this was his ground, not theirs, and was willing to threaten the Chief over it.

Was he simply protecting his case and his people? Or was there more to it?

Chief Garcia straightened. "SSA Fallon, I don't take orders from you, and I don't appreciate the attempt to railroad me. Out of respect for your undercover officers, we will proceed with caution, but I won't stop looking for Ms. Morrison simply to save your investigation. Working together is our best option, and I encourage you to reconsider my offer to do so."

Fallon looked ready to spit nails. "I'll assign an ATF agent first thing tomorrow morning. Until then, I'll need you to steer clear of the Iron Serpents. I'm sure none of us want to put my agents at risk."

"Of course not." Chief Garcia rose, a polite smile on his face. "I'm glad we could come to an agreement."

Derek scowled, the veil of politeness completely gone. He stormed out of the office, slamming the door hard behind him.

Dawson almost laughed. "Wow. Talk about a dramatic exit."

Liam grinned. "I have a feeling whoever he assigns to the task force won't be bringing donuts and coffee to our next meeting." He plopped back down in the chair. "They didn't forget to inform us about their operation. They purposefully left us out of the loop."

"The ATF should also be knocking down our door, asking for help to find Lilia." Peyton's gaze narrowed. "She dated Cade, and could be an asset. So why are they trying to hinder our investigation?"

Chief Garcia's expression was speculative as he reclaimed his seat. "It may be exactly as Fallon said. They're close to dismantling the entire organization, and they don't want us to screw that up. He didn't tell us to stop looking for Lilia, just that we needed to steer clear of Cade and the Iron Serpents."

Dawson frowned. "All this time, we've assumed Cade kidnapped Lilia from the train depot. It was a reasonable theory based on the attack on Peyton and the bandana we found at the scene. But what if she escaped and has gone underground?"

Liam tilted his head. "It could explain why we didn't find her car at the train depot."

"So... where is she? And why hasn't she contacted anyone?"

"Maybe she thinks it's too risky," Peyton suggested. "Marvis certainly sounded scared of Cade. He said he has eyes and ears everywhere..." She straightened in her chair. "Her lawyer."

Dawson frowned. "What?"

"Lilia hired an attorney to draft the guardianship paperwork for Grace. What if she knows where my cousin is? She could even have the evidence Lilia stole in her possession."

"I called her," Liam said. "Carmen Reyes refused to talk to me because of attorney-client privilege. I explained it was a matter of life and death, but she didn't budge."

"That doesn't mean anything. Lilia may have left specific instructions with her attorney, but only for me." She turned to the chief. "Not to mention, if we really believe Lilia may have escaped on the night of the train depot attack, then she's hiding out somewhere. We never figured out where she was living right before and right after having Grace. That could be where she is now. Speaking to her lawyer could be the break we need to blow this open." She grinned. "And it keeps me far away from the Iron Serpents."

Chief Garcia shot her an amused look. "You're a team player, Special Agent Hughes."

"Anything to help out the ATF, sir." She rose and arched her brows at Dawson. "What do you say, Graham? Interested in a road trip?"

He sighed. What Dawson wanted to do was lock her on his ranch behind a wall of armed guards, but he was wise enough to know he wouldn't win that argument. Peyton's mind was made up. There would be no talking her out of this. "Do I have a choice?"

She laughed, hooking an arm through his. "No. Not really."

FIFTEEN

The highway stretched ahead, nothing but farmland and fences to break up the horizon. Country music played softly from the truck's speakers. Peyton adjusted the air vent away from her face and flipped through the news articles she'd saved on her tablet. "I've been doing some research on the Iron Serpents. Their reach is a lot further than I understood—beyond Knoxville and well into Austin—and they haven't just been linked to drugs and weapons. There are several unsolved murders connected to them."

Dawson nodded, his gaze skipping to the side view mirror before focusing back on the road. His attention had been heightened since they left the police station. Knoxville was nothing but a blip behind them, but it was still another half an hour to the outskirts of Austin. Plenty of open road where they could be attacked.

Peyton leaned her head back against the seat.

"Thanks for coming with me. And for arranging protection for Grace. It means a lot."

His lips quirked. "We both know you'd be far more trouble stuck in Siberia with nothing to do but fret. Idle hands and all that."

She laughed. "I'd have Grace to keep me busy. But yes, you're right." Being trapped in a safe house would only leave her sick with worry and no way to help. She'd do it in order to protect Grace, but if there was another way to accomplish that while still working the case, she'd prefer that option. "Chief Garcia and everyone in the police department are great. Dedicated. I can see why you're happy here."

"It's home. But yes, it's nice to work with people who care as much as I do."

He'd built a life for himself. With purpose. With passion. Surrounded by coworkers, friends, and family. The only thing Peyton could see that was missing was a significant other.

The memory of their kiss wouldn't leave her alone. If the shooting, the phone call with Marvis, and learning her cousin may have stolen something from Cade hadn't kept her awake, the conversation in the barn with Dawson and their toe-curling kiss would have.

For the first time, Peyton allowed herself a tiny glimmer of hope. Hope that her cousin was alive and safe, hiding out somewhere. And hope that she and Dawson could find their way back to each other.

She longed to ask him about last night, but it was

complicated and there were more pressing matters at hand. Peyton turned back to the tablet. "Most of the murders connected to the Iron Serpents appear drug or turf related. But then I found this last night." She pulled up an article from five months ago. "An accountant named Walter Jennings was shot execution-style. His body was left on the side of the road outside north Austin. The Texas Rangers are working the case, but so far haven't developed a solid lead. Jennings was an accountant, apparently known for handling the finances of criminals. Groups like the Iron Serpents, who use legitimate businesses to launder the money they make from illegal activities."

"You think Walter Jennings's murder has something to do with Lilia?"

"I think Lilia stole something valuable from Cade, and what's more valuable than money?" She let that settle between them. "Think about it, Dawson. Lilia's life might be a mess, but she's talented mathematically. Cade knew that. Aunt Sandra mentioned he took Lilia to Vegas because she could count cards and would help him win at poker games. So years later, if Cade suspected his accountant was stealing from him, I could see him asking Lilia to look at the books."

"And what? She used the opportunity to steal money?"

"Maybe." Peyton could easily picture her cousin, desperate and pregnant, using Cade's trust against him. "She may have taken more than money. She could have evidence too. Something she could threaten Cade with in order to get him to leave her and Grace alone."

Dawson was quiet for a long moment, as if he were thinking over what she'd proposed. "It's a good theory, but we're making a lot of leaps without much evidence."

Peyton nodded. "You're right. Let's see what the attorney has to say."

The landscape changed from farmland to suburbs and then the city. Office buildings blocked out the sun as Dawson carefully navigated through downtown to a parking garage across the street from the lawyer's office. As they walked to the high-rise, his hand came to rest on the small of her back. The touch, even through her wool coat, sent awareness racing through her. Peyton edged closer to him. She was armed and kept her attention on her surroundings, but danger could come out of nowhere.

Thankfully, none found them.

They entered the lobby, went through security, and a few minutes later, were seated across from Carmen Reyes. Mid-forties, dressed in an elegant maroon suit and understated jewelry, she had the quiet composure that came from years of navigating difficult conversations. Her office was modest but immaculate—a family law degree on the wall, a framed photo of two kids on the desk, and a small succulent that looked far healthier than anything Peyton had ever kept alive.

"I explained to the detective that I spoke with yesterday, my conversations with Lilia are privileged." Carmen folded her hands on her desk. "As such, I cannot share with you anything we discussed without her express permission."

She wasn't stonewalling to be difficult. Attorney-client privilege was a serious matter, one that continued even after the client died. Peyton's heart sank. "I had hoped Lilia had left special instructions for me."

Carmen tilted her head as if puzzled. "I'm sorry, she didn't."

"Are you sure? There's no package or a letter?"

"No."

Peyton did her best to push her disappointment aside. She'd planned for this contingency. If she couldn't get her hands on the evidence, maybe they could figure out if Cade was actually Grace's father. Peyton suspected he was, but that wasn't proof. She pulled the legal documents from her bag. "That's quite all right, Mrs. Reyes. Since you drafted the guardianship document, I was hoping you could answer a few questions about it."

"I can certainly try."

She flipped to the second page and pointed to a relevant section. "Grace's father isn't listed. In fact, it says here that he's unknown."

"That's not as uncommon as one might think. Speaking in generalities, there are times a client may not wish to name the father. He could be abusive, or not in the picture, or sometimes unknown. Whenever this is the case, I take care in explaining to my clients that should something happen to them and the guardianship paperwork is triggered, the father of the child could step forward to challenge it."

"Did Lilia seem concerned about that happening? Grace's father coming forward?"

Carmen's expression didn't change, but something

shifted behind her eyes. "I can't speak to my client's state of mind. What I can tell you is that the document was drafted with care. The provisions are thorough and legally sound."

"Was she scared?"

"I cannot say."

Dawson shifted in his chair. "Can you tell us when Lilia contacted you to draft the document?"

"That's privileged."

"What about where she was living?"

"Also privileged."

He blew out a breath of frustration, and Peyton briefly laid a hand on his arm before turning to face the attorney. "Mrs. Reyes, I understand we're putting you in a difficult situation, but my cousin is missing. She's in trouble, and I'm not being melodramatic to say this is a matter of life and death. We don't know where she was living during the time of her pregnancy, or who she may have interacted with. All we have is an old Austin address, a birth record for Grace, and this guardianship paperwork. Anything you could share with us that might help our investigation would be appreciated."

Carmen met her gaze. Regret pinched her mouth. "I'm very sorry, Special Agent Hughes, but my hands are tied. The only questions I can answer for you are about the document you hold in your hand. I can also answer general legal questions. Anything more, anything specific to Lilia, is privileged."

Disappointment drew Peyton's shoulders down.

They wouldn't get anything useful out of the meeting. She rose. "I understand. Thank you for your time."

"Certainly." Carmen shook Peyton's hand and then Dawson's.

They started for the door. Dawson reached it first, holding it open for Peyton. She was just about to cross the threshold when Carmen said, "Special Agent Hughes."

Peyton turned.

"I'm sorry. It was terribly rude of me not to ask. How is Grace?"

"She misses her mother."

Carmen nodded, her expression a mix of understanding and sympathy. "Becoming a guardian unexpectedly can be nerve-wracking, and learning to take care of an infant can be overwhelming. There's a wonderful parenting class held at Saint Andrew's Church. They also run a women's shelter, which is always in need of donations if you feel so inclined. Ask for Mimi Nguyen. She can help you."

Peyton's heart skipped a beat. She held the other woman's gaze for a moment, doing her best to convey the gratitude swelling in her chest. "Thank you, counselor."

"Good luck, Special Agent. I hope you find Lilia safe and sound."

"So do I."

SIXTEEN

Saint Andrew's Church was three blocks away, tucked between towering office buildings like a relic from a bygone era. Mimi Nguyen, the director of operations, was currently running an errand but would be back soon. The secretary invited them to wait in the church. Pews lined either side of the aisle leading to the marble altar. Vaulted ceilings soared overhead, and stained-glass windows painted the stone floor in shifting colors as the sun moved across the sky. Dawson was humbled by it.

"Gorgeous," Peyton murmured, her neck craning to take in the carvings on the giant stone columns. Her steps were silent as she gravitated to the piano tucked in the corner, near a set of risers probably used for the choir. She touched the wood lovingly before lifting her attention to the cross hanging behind the pulpit.

Dawson's chest tightened. He'd spent hours watching her play the piano in church. In those moments, she'd lose herself, completely unguarded, her mind and spirit taken over by the music. It'd been a beautiful sight to witness. One of the many things he missed.

She'd stopped playing entirely after Samuel died.

"Do you miss it?" Dawson joined her. He'd removed his cowboy hat and held it loosely in one hand.

Peyton's brows crinkled in confusion for a moment, and then understanding dawned. "I started playing in church last year. Not consistently. Work keeps me busy, but I play as much as I can."

"What made you return to it?"

She turned to face him. "Remember when I told you I was in a bad car accident? It was about a year and a half ago. My fault. I was working overtime, not taking care of myself, and I fell asleep at the wheel. Just for a moment. But it was long enough to send my patrol car over the curb. It flipped three times. The doctor said it was a miracle I survived."

He inhaled sharply. She'd nearly died, and he hadn't known about it.

"I couldn't understand it." Peyton tucked a strand of hair behind her ear, her gaze lifting to the cross once again. "Why had God spared me? It didn't make sense. For years, I'd believed that He was punishing me. That losing Samuel was proof that I wasn't worthy of true happiness."

It hurt to hear her say these things about herself. Dawson had known that Peyton struggled with self-esteem long before their son's death. She'd been through so much even before they met. A father who abandoned her, a mother who loved her but had been chaotic and unstable until her death. Nana Grace had been a steadying force, but even that had been fraught with trouble. Sandra's battle with addiction had affected the whole family, including Lilia, who floated back and forth between her mother and her grandmother.

Peyton had responded to the chaos by excelling in every way she could. In her studies. In music. On the softball field. And it dawned on him. "You tried to earn God's love."

She nodded. "After the accident, I wanted to understand why, if I was so unworthy, had God spared me? I went to church for the first time since Samuel died. The pastor helped me see that my faith had been transactional, but that's not how it works. God doesn't love me because I earned it. He loves me because I'm His. That's it. That's enough."

The words were heartfelt and reverent. They pierced Dawson's heart with their truth. He'd noticed a shift in her, a peace and quiet confidence that hadn't been there before. Now he understood it.

He reached for her hand, taking it in his and squeezing lightly. "I'm glad you found your way back to Him, Peyton."

Their eyes met, and a thousand unspoken words passed between them. Gratitude. Regret. Loss. Hope. They didn't need to say any of it. Fifteen years of loving someone gave you a language that didn't require words.

A door creaked open, interrupting the quiet moment, followed by brisk footsteps. Moments later, an older woman with gray hair and reading glasses hanging from a chain around her neck appeared. Dawson dropped Peyton's hand and turned to greet her. "Mimi Nguyen?"

"Yes." She came to a stop in front of them, her assessing gaze cataloging Peyton and then Dawson.

Mimi might look like someone's kind grandmother, but she had the careful astuteness of a woman who'd spent years sizing up strangers and deciding whether they could be trusted.

Dawson shifted his jacket so his badge was visible. "I'm Detective Dawson Graham with the Knoxville Police Department. This is Special Agent Peyton Hughes. We were hoping you could answer a few questions about Lilia Morrison." It was on the tip of his tongue to say that Carmen Reyes had sent them, but he didn't want to get the lawyer into trouble. Technically, she hadn't violated attorney-client privilege, but she'd skittered very close to it. "Lilia is missing, and it's important that we find her. Peyton is her cousin."

Mimi clasped her hands in front of her. "Forgive me, Detective Graham, but I don't know a Lilia Morrison."

She was lying. Dawson held her gaze. "Call the Knoxville Police Department and ask for Chief Sam Garcia. He will confirm our investigation and verify we are who we say we are."

Mimi tilted her head, studying him for a moment, and then gestured to a collection of chairs in the corner. "Have a seat and give me a moment."

She moved away from them, pulling a cell phone from her pocket. Dawson steered Peyton toward the chairs with a light touch.

"She's cautious," Peyton whispered.

"Mimi runs a women's shelter. She won't give out information about a client without verifying our identities. And even then, we may not get much out of her. It's frustrating, but I understand it. The women she's protecting have been abused, and many of them don't trust law enforcement or the courts to protect them. I'd be more surprised if she wasn't cautious." Dawson claimed a chair next to Peyton. "She didn't recognize your name."

"No." Worry clouded Peyton's hazel eyes, and her shoulders were tense. "Do you think Lilia is hiding in the shelter?"

"Maybe. But if so, why hasn't she called you?"

Dawson feared Lilia was dead. Or being held by someone. Maybe SSA Fallon's intel wasn't as thorough as he liked to believe. Or he could've been lying to them. Dawson didn't like the idea that a federal agent was actively misleading them, but the Iron Serpents had connections in law enforcement. It explained how they'd been able to operate for so long without being shut down.

Mimi hung up and approached, her long dress swirling around her legs. Some of the tension in her posture was gone, and as she sat, her demeanor was more open and friendly. "Forgive me, Detective Graham. Special Agent Hughes. I hope you understand, but in my line of work, I can't afford to take people at their word. The women in my care depend on me to be their first line of defense. Chief Garcia confirmed your investigation, and I'd like to help in any way I can."

"Do you know where Lilia is?" Peyton asked.

"No, I'm sorry, I don't. She left our shelter last week and I haven't heard from her since." Worry creased the space between her brows. "It was my understanding she was taking Grace to stay with family. You, in fact."

Surprise flickered through Dawson. So Mimi had recognized Peyton's name after all. He prided himself on being able to read people, but in this case, Mimi could give lessons on hiding her true thoughts. "What day was this?"

"She left Thursday morning."

"In her car?"

"Yes, a 1999 Toyota Camry. Light blue." She frowned. "You said Lilia is missing? Since when?"

Peyton quickly detailed the desperate phone call from Lilia and the attack at the train depot. "As you can imagine, we're very concerned for her safety. According to my aunt, Lilia was dating Cade Maddox, the leader of a biker gang."

Mimi nodded. "She moved in with Cade last year, shortly after falling pregnant. Initially, Lilia didn't know about Cade's criminal activities, but it soon became clear that he was more than a bar owner. By then, he'd isolated her from everyone, and the abuse had begun. Lilia was scared for her life, and that of her unborn child."

Peyton closed her eyes, her expression pained. "So Cade is Grace's father?"

"Yes, and she was terrified he would find them. It took a lot of courage for Lilia to leave."

Dawson could only imagine. "What made her decide to contact Peyton? Did Cade find her?"

"No." Mimi clasped her hands in her lap. "When Lilia left, she stole money from Cade, along with evidence of his criminal activities. Initially, she'd intended to keep it as insurance, to prevent Cade from coming after her and Grace. But once her daughter was born, she had second thoughts." Mimi looked directly at Peyton. "She wanted to do the right thing and come forward. We discussed the matter, and I offered to help her go to the police, but she didn't want to make any moves without making sure Grace was taken care of first. It was my understanding that she was going to confess everything to you and ask you to protect her baby. That's why she had the guardianship paperwork drawn up."

"Something went wrong," Peyton pressed her fingers to her forehead. "Somehow Cade—or someone else in the Iron Serpents—figured out what she was up to and ambushed her at the train depot before I arrived." She dropped her hand. "Whoever is behind this wants the money and the evidence."

Dawson nodded, placing a reassuring hand on her knee before turning back to Mimi. "Do you have a copy of the evidence Lilia stole? Or do you know where it is?"

"No, I don't. She never showed it to me."

"Can we see where she was staying?" Dawson wondered if Lilia had hidden some place in the women's shelter.

"That would be impossible. Lilia cleaned out her

room when she left, and someone else is living there now."

Dawson and Peyton asked a few more questions, but it quickly became clear Mimi had told them everything she could. As the interview came to a close, Dawson handed her his card. "If you hear from Lilia, or think of anything that might help our investigation, please call me. Day or night."

"I will." Mimi stepped forward and embraced Peyton. When she pulled away, there were tears in her eyes. "Please, if you can, let me know what happens. Lilia and Grace have been in my prayers since they left, but I'll ask God to guide the investigation as well." She reached out to pat Dawson on the arm. "Stay safe. All of you."

They thanked her. As they moved toward the exit of the church, two questions circled Dawson's mind.

Where was Lilia?

And where was the evidence?

Sunshine beat down on his shoulders as they stepped outside. Dawson settled his cowboy hat on his head. He'd left his truck in the parking garage across the street from the lawyer's office. A snarl of traffic blocked the road, the blare of horns punctuating the afternoon air.

Peyton zipped up her coat. Her expression was heartbroken. "I thought we'd find her here."

"I know." He wanted to take away her worries. Protect her. But if there was anything Samuel's death had taught him, it was that some things couldn't be fixed by sheer strength of will. "We're doing the best we can,

Peyton. That's all we can ask of ourselves. The rest has to be left up to God."

She squeezed his hand. "Yes. You're right." Peyton released a long breath. "I'm starving. What do you say we grab a bite to eat and discuss a game plan? I was thinking—"

The sound of a motorcycle drowned out her sentence. Dawson reacted automatically, yanking Peyton behind a large column. Adrenaline slammed through him. The sound of the motorcycles grew louder, the engines revving. Peyton froze. He held up a hand, showing she should stay in place, and then peeked around the rounded curve of the column.

On the street, weaving through the traffic, were two members of the Iron Serpents. They drove slowly, their eyes sweeping the sidewalks and buildings.

They were searching. Hunting.

For them.

SEVENTEEN

Peyton's muscles coiled with tension. Dawson's body blocked her sight, but the rumble of the motorcycles was unmistakable. "Iron Serpents?"

"Yes. They're looking for us." A muscle in his jaw worked. "It might not be safe to go back to my truck. I don't know how they found us."

Peyton's mind raced. They hadn't been followed from Knoxville, she was sure of it. No one knew they were coming to Austin except the team at the police station. So how—

The lawyer's office.

She lightly touched Dawson's arm, leaning over to catch a glimpse of the men on the motorcycles. A shiver raced down her spine. "Carmen Reyes. Someone was watching her office and saw us go in. Maybe they tried to follow us to the church, but we lost them along the way."

Dawson held up a finger and then took her hand in

his. Keeping his attention locked on the street, he tugged her across the pavement toward the church. Together, they slipped back inside. Dawson positioned them behind a wall, but used the glass doors to keep watch. "How would Cade even know about Carmen?"

"The guardianship paperwork. Child Protective Services filed it with the family court when they placed Grace in my custody. Carmen's name is on the filing as the drafting attorney." Peyton's stomach dropped. "All Cade needed was a lawyer with access to the family court database, and he'd have Carmen's name and her office address. Everything. He's been keeping watch, hoping Lilia would show back up here. Instead, he found us. And he's trailing us, hoping that we'll lead him straight to my cousin. Or the evidence. Or both."

It cemented the notion that Cade didn't have Lilia. Her cousin was being held by someone else or had gone underground and was hiding. Frustration swelled. This case had been one confusing twist after another, and even several days in, it felt like they were still working with half the picture.

Dawson stiffened, his fingers flying to his holstered weapon. Peyton eased around him to see a member of the Iron Serpents approaching the building on foot. In seconds they would be found, and exchanging gunfire in a church might get people killed. Grabbing his wrist, she pulled him across the narthex and into the church. Mimi was still there, rearranging the flowers around the altar. She glanced up, startled, as they ran toward her.

"Is there a rear exit?" Peyton's words were clipped.

"Come with me." Mimi led them to a side door and down a long hallway. She disabled an alarm before pushing open the arm on an emergency exit. It dumped them into a narrow alley. She pointed to the left. "There is a set of back streets. Four blocks southeast is the police department."

"Bless you." Peyton lightly touched her arm. "You never saw us."

"Understood. Godspeed, child."

Dawson, his weapon unholstered but held by his side, took the lead. They moved quickly through the narrow alley, weaving between dumpsters and stacked pallets. The sounds of downtown Austin—traffic, voices, the distant wail of a siren—echoed off the brick walls, making it impossible to tell which direction was safe. Peyton kept one hand on her own weapon as she matched Dawson's pace.

They cut through a gap between two buildings and emerged onto a quieter side street. No motorcycles. The stench of rotten food from overflowing garbage bags caused Peyton to gag. She did her best to breathe through her nose as Dawson peeked around a corner. He waited a beat, then jerked his chin to the left. Peyton scurried across the open space, her insides shuddering when a rat crossed her path. She ducked into the safety of another alley. Dawson followed.

Three more blocks to go.

The pavement was slick with runoff from a leaking pipe, and the ground was littered with debris. Broken bottles, rusted cans, and a scattering of splintered wooden crates. The sound of a motorcycle reached her ears, and Peyton's head whipped around, searching for the source. Fear, thick and intense, shot through her as a dark shadow crossed the street they'd just turned off of. They were closing in. The memory of what Dawson had told her when they arrived at Sidewinders replayed in her mind.

These guys could shoot us, and all of them would lie about what happened. They'll say whatever they're told.

Her foot caught the edge of a shattered pallet, and she went down hard, throwing her hands out to break the fall. Pain—white-hot and blinding—lanced through her side. She gasped and looked down. A jagged hole had been ripped through her jacket. She couldn't see what had cut her, but she felt blood seeping through the thin fabric of her undershirt.

"Peyton." Dawson was at her side in an instant.

"I'm okay," she lied. There was no time for first aid. The rumble of motorcycles was growing louder, nearly vibrating the ground underneath her. She pressed her free hand to her side as Dawson hauled her to her feet. Gritting her teeth against the agony radiating out from the injury, she kept moving forward, her eyes locked on the entrance to the alley. Adrenaline and sheer determination fueled her steps.

Please God, help us.

They rounded the corner, and for half a heartbeat, Peyton thought they would make it. But then two motorcycles swung onto the road ahead of them. Dawson lurched to a stop, and she nearly ran into him. Automatically, as if of one mind, they whirled to go back the way they came, but three more bikes burst into the narrow road, cutting off their escape.

They were trapped.

EIGHTEEN

It hurt to breathe. Her body shook as Dawson gently pushed her behind him, positioning Peyton between a brick wall and his solid form. The math was brutal. Five bikes. At least seven men. Her heart raced, and she kept a hand clamped over the wound. Blood trailed down her skin. It was impossible to know how badly she was hurt, but the pain was enough to cloud her vision. She couldn't shoot straight even if she tried.

Dawson, wisely, kept his gun ready, but at his side. A shootout in this alley would end badly for them.

The engines cut out one by one. Silence pressed in, somehow worse than the noise. Boots scraped against the pavement as the riders dismounted.

Then a familiar voice echoed off the brick walls.

"Princess Peyton." Cade stepped through the line of his men, hands in his pockets, as unhurried as if he were strolling through his own bar. His dark eyes found hers over Dawson's shoulder, and that predatory smile spread across his face. "We meet again."

Anger flared, hot enough to momentarily cut through the pain. Peyton sidestepped Dawson and jutted up her chin. "Are you following me, Cade?"

"I'm protecting you. You never know what bad things can happen in back alleys."

He jerked his chin, and within seconds, Peyton and Dawson were grabbed. She cried out as rough hands disarmed her before searching her pockets. Someone removed her cell phone and her backup weapon. The roaring in her ears blocked out the sound of Dawson calling her name. One of Cade's men punched him in the stomach, and he doubled over.

"Stop!" Peyton struggled against the hands that held her. Her purse strap broke, and the contents tumbled onto the cement. Ricky bent down and sifted through items before shoving his thick fingers into every compartment. The spider tattoo on his neck swam as dark spots clouded the edge of her vision. Peyton feared she'd throw up.

Ricky threw down her bag. "They don't have it, boss."

Dawson struggled to his feet, only to be grabbed and held back. His expression was thunderous, his breathing shallow. Blood trickled from a cut on his lip. Peyton belatedly realized he'd taken more than one hit. Fear—not for herself, but for Dawson—nearly buckled her knees. If Cade perceived Dawson as a threat, he wouldn't hesitate to kill him. She needed to keep Cade's attention on her. All of it.

"You're going down, Cade." Dawson's voice rang out with authority. "If it's the last thing I do, I'm gonna put you behind bars."

Cade ignored him, his attention locked on Peyton. "We need to talk." He spun on his heel and moved a short distance away.

The hands holding Peyton in place released her. She briefly met Dawson's gaze, silently willing him to simmer down. They needed to focus on getting out of this alive.

And then she would help Dawson snap the handcuffs on Cade's wrists herself.

Limping slightly, doing her best to ignore the fiery agony in her side, she joined Cade near the rusted carcass of an overturned shopping cart. Putting a touch of amusement into her voice, she said, "If you wanted to talk, all you had to do was call."

Cade's expression remained flat. "You and I share a common interest."

Peyton didn't believe for a second that he was talking about her cousin. "You mean Grace."

"Yes." His attention darted to the men guarding Dawson, and his mouth tightened. "Someone is trying to bury me."

"That's what happens when you're a criminal."

He sneered. "Don't be cute. My enemies are looking for Lilia and the evidence she stole. They want to use it against me, and they'll kill anyone standing in their way. You." His head jerked toward Dawson. "That idiot over there. Even Grace, if they think it'll destroy me."

Peyton raised her brows. "You expect me to believe that you care about what happens to Grace."

"She's my child." The words were spoken matter-of-factly. Bluntly. As if it were obvious that a cold-blooded killer would move heaven and earth to protect his daughter. Cade stared at Peyton. "You may not like me, but you can count on this. I'll do what's necessary to protect what's mine."

The raw possessiveness in his voice made her sick. Grace was a human being, not something to be owned and controlled. And yet, a part of Peyton recognized that for him, this was as close to expressing love as Cade would probably ever get.

Her brain was getting muddled and fuzzy. The blood soaking her shirt was turning cold, and goosebumps broke out across her skin. "What do you want?"

"Lose your bodyguard and bring Grace to Sidewinders where I can protect you both."

Her gaze narrowed. "How can you do that? Rumor has it someone inside your own gang is trying to take you down." She got into his space. "I know about Marvis."

"I'm handling it."

"Then Grace would already be safe." Peyton wanted out of this situation alive, but she also sensed that if she was too conciliatory, Cade's paranoia would take over. It was a fine line to walk, but it was still there. "You don't want to protect Grace. You want to use her and me to flush Lilia out so she'll give you the evidence. But guess what? I protect what's mine too, and I won't be used as a tool to hurt her. So let's work out a deal."

He grabbed her arm. She nearly screamed when pain erupted from her wound as he yanked her toward him. Cade got into her face, his nose nearly touching hers. "Give me one good reason why I shouldn't shoot you right here?"

The anger in his eyes iced her to the core, but Peyton refused to look away. "Because I'm the best chance you have of finding what Lilia stole. And we both know that's really what you want."

He chuckled. His grip on her arm tightened. "And you'll give it to me? Just like that?"

She nodded. "In exchange for your promise that you won't hurt Grace, Lilia, or anyone else I care about."

It was a calculated risk. She had no intention of actually following through, but Cade couldn't know that. Otherwise, he might shoot them right here and be done with it.

His fingers pressed into her flesh, practically rubbing against the bone. She held his gaze, not letting an ounce of pain or fear flicker across her expression. As a poker player, Cade was used to reading other people's bluffs. If this was going to work, she had to sell it. Not with words. With confidence.

He countered her silent challenge with his own, whipping out his gun and holding it to her throat. "If you're lying to me, I will kill you."

"I know."

Ricky edged forward. "Easy, boss. They're cops, and we've got enough problems to deal with."

Cade's gaze never flickered to his subordinate.

Instead, he pushed Peyton away, finally releasing her arm. Before she could find her footing, his hand collided with her cheekbone. Stars exploded in her vision. She collapsed to the ground in a bone-jarring heap that ripped a scream from her throat.

Above her, barely visible through the haze of pain, Cade smirked. Then he waved a hand. "Load up!"

Movement out of the corner of her eye preceded a clatter against the asphalt. Her cell phone and guns. Seconds later, the motorcycle engines fired. Peyton could barely hear them through the dull roaring of pain in her ears. Dawson's face swam in front of her. She tried to speak, to explain her side was bleeding badly, but the words wouldn't come. The stars in her vision grew bigger, darker.

And as she slipped into the darkness, all she could think was that she'd done it.

She'd protected Dawson.

It worked. He's safe.

NINETEEN

Dawson prowled the emergency room waiting area. His stomach, already sour with worry and fear, turned at the stench of antiseptic and bleach. After passing out in the alley, Peyton had come to in the ambulance, but she'd quickly been whisked away the moment they arrived at the emergency room. Security hadn't allowed him past the swinging doors, not even after he flashed his badge. Austin wasn't his jurisdiction.

An hour had gone by. Still nothing.

Dawson couldn't stay still. He marched to the nurse's station. "Peyton Hughes. How is she?"

"Sir, I've already told you, when there's news, the doctor will come and update you." The nurse's glare was sharp enough to cut to the bone. "If you approach this desk one more time, I'll have security escort you to the parking lot. Are we clear?"

He wanted to scream. Instead, he gave her a sharp

nod, not trusting himself to say anything that wouldn't get him thrown out. As he turned away from the nurses' station, the main doors to the hospital slid open. Jax strolled in. Some of the emotional turmoil rolling through Dawson settled at the sight of his childhood friend.

"How is she?" Jax asked, meeting Dawson near an empty group of chairs.

"I don't know. They won't tell me anything." His hands balled into fists. "Cade's goons chased us, and as we were trying to get away, Peyton fell. She must've stabbed herself somehow. She told me she was fine, but she wasn't. Then Cade ambushed us, and it turns out she was bleeding the entire time."

Those harrowing moments in the alley kept playing on a loop he couldn't stop. Cade, putting his hands on her. The gun at her throat. The slap. Dawson had never felt such rage in his entire life. He hadn't known it was possible. And then... when Peyton passed out... and he'd opened her jacket and saw the blood...

The fear had nearly undone him.

His knees buckled, and he collapsed into a plastic chair. Dawson hung his head in his hands. "Cade was going to kill us. You could feel it, you know? But Peyton talked to him, made some kind of deal, and he let us go."

"What kind of deal?"

"I don't know yet. When she came to in the ambulance, all she would say was not to arrest Cade."

Tears pricked the back of his eyes. Whatever magic trick she'd pulled had saved both their lives. He'd spent their entire marriage believing he was the one to safeguard her, but it was finally dawning on him that Peyton had never needed his protection. She needed his support. His attention. His communication.

She needed them to be a team.

Dawson lifted his head and focused on his best friend. "Do you think I hold my feelings in? Like when I'm mad or upset?"

Jax arched his brows. "Yeah, dude."

He hung his head again. Jax settled into the seat next to him. Long moments stretched in silence. Somewhere in the waiting room, a baby cried and was then shushed by its mother. Dawson knew he should pray, but he couldn't find the words. He just... couldn't.

"I'm in love with Peyton." The words came out in a whisper. He'd tried to avoid it, tried to lie to himself about it, but the truth was, he'd always loved her. And maybe always would.

"Okay, Captain Obvious. Is there anything else you'd like to share? I hold my feelings in, I'm in love with my ex, the sky is blue—"

"Seriously?" Dawson glowered at his friend. "Are you actually cracking jokes now?"

Jax held up his hands in the classic sign of surrender. "It's been clear from the moment Peyton showed up in Knoxville that you weren't over her." He paused. "Well, honestly, I knew that *before* she showed up. But you get the point. Why do you think I tried to talk you out of bringing her to your family's ranch?"

"Does everyone know I'm in love with her?"

"Everyone with eyes."

Dawson groaned.

Jax clapped him on the back. "If it makes you feel any better, I'm pretty sure she's still in love with you too."

His heart skipped a beat. But it was followed by a forbidding sense of fear. "What difference does it make? She left me once. What's stopping her from doing it again?"

"Sounds like a good question for Peyton."

"Do you think she knows the answer? Neither of us expected to lose Samuel, or to have our marriage fall apart." Dawson stared at hands, at the empty left ring finger. "We made promises. Vows to each other in front of our family and in the eyes of God. If that didn't hold us together, what will?"

Jax was quiet for a long moment. "You're right. Vows didn't hold you together. But you were also kids when you made them. Barely out of college, no idea what life was about to throw at you." He leaned forward, resting his elbows on his knees. "The question isn't whether Peyton will leave again. You can't control that. The question is whether the woman sitting in that emergency room is the same woman who walked out on you five years ago."

"She's not." Dawson knew that. He'd seen it. Felt it.

"And you're not either. You've both grown. Changed. Learned from your mistakes."

They had. But was it enough? Dawson wasn't sure. And he knew loving anyone required a leap of faith, but this... it felt... bigger somehow. More risky.

Probably because he knew just how painful it would be if it all fell apart again.

Dawson tilted his head, curiosity getting the better of him. "I thought you'd be completely against me getting back with Peyton."

Jax extended his feet in front of him. "I was. At first. But I dunno, man. There's something about the two of you that just works." He shrugged his shoulders. "And honestly, who am I to judge? I hated Megan for years before falling in love with her. She helped me understand that people can grow and change, become better. Everyone deserves a second chance."

A second chance. He liked the sound of that.

Dawson sat back in his chair. Time ticked by slowly. Patients came and went, ambulances screamed in and then left in a whirl of activity. Jax fetched coffee for them both, but Dawson couldn't drink his. He left it sitting on the small, white table next to him. None of it mattered. Not right now. His gaze stayed locked on the doors leading to the interior of the emergency room. He didn't know what to feel, or how to make sense of anything that was happening. All he knew was that he loved Peyton and wanted her to be okay.

Finally, the door swung open, and a doctor emerged. "Detective Graham?"

"That's me." Dawson shot out of his seat and closed the distance in three strides.

"Special Agent Hughes is asking for you."

A wave of relief washed over him. "How is she?"

The doctor led him down a hall, past a hectic nurses'

station and people waiting on beds in the hallway. "The gash on her side needed stitches, and she'll need a tetanus shot since we're not sure what caused the laceration. She'll make a full recovery."

A nurse called out to the doctor, distracting him. He pointed to the last cubicle. "Right there. Bed 15." Then he was gone in a flutter of a lab coat.

Dawson weaved his way through people, his chest tight and his heart pounding. The beds were sectioned off with nothing but a curtain. Peyton's was at the end, and as he rounded the corner, she came into view. He pulled up short at the sight.

Her hair was a tangled mess, half-fallen from its ponytail. Blood stained the front of her shirt in a dark, uneven bloom. A bruise was already deepening across her cheekbone where Cade had struck her. She was perched on the edge of the bed, struggling to feed her arm through the sleeve of her jacket, wincing with every movement.

Then she looked up. And smiled. Not a small, polite, I'm-fine smile. A full, radiant, light-up-the-room smile that hit him like a punch to the chest.

"There you are. I told them to go get you an hour ago, but they kept insisting on..."

He didn't hear anything she said after that. Dawson closed the distance between them, cupped her face in his shaking hands, and kissed her.

His lips were warm, his touch gentle, and Peyton sank into the kiss. Warmth spread through her. She reached up and curled her fingers into the front of his shirt. Pulling him closer. Needing him closer. The sounds of the ER drifted away until there was nothing but them, cocooned in a world of their own making. Dawson's hands trembled against her cheeks, and she felt everything he couldn't say in the pressure of his fingers, the way he held her as if she might disappear.

They'd shared hundreds of kisses throughout their courtship. Some had been tender, some passionate, some fun. But few had held the depth of feeling this one did. As if the near-death experiences over the last few days had burned through every wall, every excuse, every reason they'd told themselves this was over, and revealed what had been underneath the whole time.

Love.

She loved him. Always had. Probably always would. And Peyton believed deep down that Dawson still loved her. It was there, in his touch. In his kiss.

Where did that leave them? She didn't know.

They couldn't move forward until they left their old mistakes in the past.

Dawson brushed his lips against hers once more before lifting his head to look her in the eyes. "You are either the bravest woman I've ever met or the most reckless." His mouth quirked up at the corner, making him seem both boyish and charming. "I'm thinking it's a bit of both."

She scowled, but there was no real heat behind it.

"Look in a mirror, pal. You practically dared Cade to shoot you on the spot with that arrest talk."

"Yeah, that wasn't smart." His thumb brushed across her bruised cheek. Soft. Gentle. "I don't know what kind of deal you made with Cade, but it saved both our lives."

"I promised to give whatever Lilia stole to him when I find it."

Dawson stilled. "And he bought it?"

She shrugged, wincing as the movement pulled on her stitches. "He's desperate. There's a mutiny happening within his own ranks, and I sense he knows about the federal investigation into the Iron Serpents. He might be able to survive all of that, but only if he gets his hands on what Lilia stole." She played with a button on Dawson's shirt. "You didn't put out an arrest warrant, did you?"

"No." Dawson eased himself down next to Peyton on the bed. "Jax is outside in the waiting room. He'll escort us back to Knoxville, make sure we don't run into any more trouble. Chief Garcia has been advised of the situation, but as you requested, I asked him to hold off on arresting Cade until I talked to you."

Peyton breathed out. "Thank you. If we arrest Cade now, his organization fragments. Marvis or someone else takes over, and we lose any chance of finding Lilia. Worse, we blow the ATF's undercover operation. Cade thinks I made a deal with him. Let him believe it. As long as he believes I'm going to deliver the evidence, he has a reason to keep us alive and stay visible. The moment we arrest him, we lose that leverage." She paused. "I'm pretty sure Ricky is an undercover cop, by the way."

"I came to the same conclusion. He pinged my internal sensors at Sidewinders, but I couldn't place why. After we met with SSA Fallon, I started wondering if he was the undercover agent. Today's search of your bag confirmed it. Street criminals dump and sift. Ricky's technique was textbook law enforcement—systematic, thorough, every compartment. And then when Cade put a gun to your throat, Ricky reached for his own weapon. His instinct was to protect you. But he couldn't blow his cover, so he did the next best thing by trying to convince Cade to back off."

Dawson's assessment matched her own. "Cade confirmed Marvis is challenging him for power. He may not be the only one though, so we should be careful." She grimaced. "I assume Marvis hasn't been found yet?"

"You assume correctly."

She tried to put her jacket on, but the sleeve wouldn't cooperate and a shooting pain creased her side. Only five stitches at her waist, but they hurt with every move. "Everyone is searching for what Lilia stole. We have to find it. And her."

"I agree, but where could she be?"

"I have an idea about that, but I'll need your help to pull it off."

"Anything you need."

She grinned, abandoning her jacket to hook a finger in his shirt and pull him down for a kiss. Her heart tumbled as desire darkened his eyes. "Anything I need?" Peyton loved the way his breath hitched in response.

Then his gaze narrowed. "It's not gonna require me to tangle with any more criminal bikers, is it?"

She chuckled. "Well... maybe one." Before he could ask anything more, she kissed him again and then said, "Help me put on my jacket, Dawson, and then I'll tell you my plan."

TWENTY

Two hours later, Peyton popped a piece of candy into her mouth and flipped to the next page of Marvis Harrison's criminal file. She'd borrowed a desk at the Knoxville Police Department, and the stack of paperwork in front of her painted a picture that was far more troubling than she'd expected.

On paper, Marvis Harrison looked like a garden-variety thug, but the deeper Peyton dug, the more the pattern shifted. Every arrest had been plea-bargained down, and the sentences reduced. Witnesses recanted. Evidence went missing. He'd even skated out of a second-degree murder charge when the only witness disappeared two days before trial. He was either the luckiest criminal in Texas, or he was far more dangerous than he initially appeared.

Dawson leaned over the wall of her cubicle and stole a candy. "Whatcha working on?"

"Looking into Marvis. He's smart and crafty, but

according to our information, he hasn't belonged to the Iron Serpents for very long. So how has he been able to challenge Cade for leadership? It didn't make sense to me. Until I found this." She rummaged through some papers and pulled one out. "Larry Owens was the original boss of the Iron Serpents. Well, guess what? Marvis is his son."

Dawson whistled. "Wow. How did we miss this?"

"It took a while to connect the dots. Marvis was raised by his mother in Waco. The only connection I found was buried in a decade-old arrest report from when Marvis was eighteen. His mother listed Larry Owens as his biological father on the emergency contact form." She tapped the paper in Dawson's hand. "After Larry died, Cade took over. But if Marvis believes leadership should have passed to him by blood, that could cause a turf war."

Dawson took another candy, his expression darkening. "It would also split the gang members. Some would agree that Larry's son has a rightful claim."

"Exactly. I don't believe for a second Marvis was telling the truth about being ordered to kidnap Grace. He was acting on his own behalf. He wants to take Cade down." Peyton shifted carefully in her chair, the stitches pulling.

Propped up on the desk was an arrest photo of Marvis. Lanky, with unevenly cut brown hair and boyish cheeks, he looked like a mischievous teen. Disarming and harmless. But the cold calculation behind his dark eyes was all too familiar. She'd seen that look before in experienced criminals. The blue and red tattoo on his neck was fully visible in the mugshot, a serpent coiled around a dagger.

A shudder raced across her skin. It was terrifying to think this man had nearly gotten his hands on Grace.

Dawson's attention drifted to the windows overlooking the parking lot as he stole another piece of her candy. She smacked his hand away but was too late to save her chocolate. He jerked his chin. "Looks like your plan worked."

She rose and turned in time to see the front doors of the police department fly open.

"You can't do this! He has rights!" Sandra's angry voice bellowed across the bullpen as she followed her boyfriend, Bobby, who was being escorted in handcuffs. The Iron Serpent member sported a fresh scrape on his chin and a nasty scowl. Tucker held a tight grip on the man's arm. His uniform was wrinkled, his shirt half untucked.

Trailing behind the group was Liam. His cowboy hat was missing, and mud stained the front of his shirt. He glowered at Peyton and Dawson. "Bobby ran. We had to chase him clear across the trailer park." He lifted a set of clear evidence bags. One held white pills and the other a gun. "He had these on him."

Sandra, blocked from following Bobby to the holding cell by Hayley, whirled to face Peyton. Her expression was thunderous, the scent of gin and desperation pouring from her. "Did you do this, Princess Peyton?" Her words slurred. "You set Bobby up, didn't you? He was just minding his own business."

Liam rolled his eyes. "He was doing fifty in a school zone."

"Everyone speeds there!" Sandra was moving from angry to irate, and as she stepped up aggressively toward the detective, Peyton stepped between them.

"Come with me, Aunt Sandra. Maybe there's something I can do to help Bobby get out of this mess." She steered her aunt toward an interview room, noting the dirty bandage on Sandra's wrist and the dark bruise along her jaw. Anger twisted her insides, but she kept her tone even. "It looks like you got hurt recently. Do you need to see a doctor?"

Sandra's gaze skittered away as she tossed her tote bag on the table and mumbled, "I fell. I'm fine."

A lie. Bobby was beating her. But Peyton was wise enough to let the matter drop. She needed her aunt's cooperation, and accusing her deadbeat boyfriend of more crimes wasn't the way to do it. Instead, she asked, "Can I get you some water? Or a soda?"

"A soda. Cold." She rummaged around in her bag. "And a cup."

Peyton rolled her eyes, already knowing where this was going, but did her aunt's bidding anyway. When she came out of the break room, Dawson was waiting next to the interrogation room door. Broad-shouldered and more handsome than any man had a right to be. Her breath caught when their gazes met, and the memory of their kiss in the hospital a few hours ago rose unbidden in her mind.

A distraction. One she couldn't indulge in.

"Need me to go in with you?" His dark eyes held sympathy, but no pity.

"No. I think she'll say more if it's just the two of us." Peyton smiled, touched that he asked. "But thanks for the offer."

Dawson touched her shoulder briefly. "I'll be watching from the audio-visual room." He leaned closer, his breath whispering across her earlobe. "Go get 'em, tiger."

The fierce pride in his voice warmed her straight through. She took a moment to admire the view of him walking down the hall before she drew in a breath, straightened her shoulders, and entered the interview room. Sandra had unearthed an electronic cigarette from her purse along with a crumpled water bottle that almost certainly was filled with a clear type of alcohol.

"You need to tell those cops to let Bobby go." Sandra cradled her injured wrist to her chest, watching as Peyton set the sodas down on the table with suspicion. "He didn't do nothin' wrong."

"I might be able to help him out, but I need you to answer a few questions for me first." Peyton cracked open one of the drinks and pushed it toward Sandra.

Her aunt immediately dumped some in the plastic cup and followed it up with a hearty splash of whatever was in her water bottle. "What kinda questions?"

"About Lilia."

"I already told you everything I know." Sandra threw back the drink, draining it in one go. Then she sucked on her cigarette. The stench of alcohol and synthetic vanilla from the e-cigarette mingled into something cloyingly sweet. It coated the small room like an invisible fog.

"You're lying." Peyton's tone was matter-of-fact. "If you want me to help Bobby, then you need to tell me the truth—"

"Who do you think you are, Princess Peyton?" A string of curse words so nasty they'd make a seasoned soldier blush flew out of Sandra's mouth. Rage, or the alcohol, put color in her cheeks. Her sweatshirt was stained and hung off her malnourished form. She was a bully fueled by addiction and sheer hatred. "How dare you accuse me of lying about my daughter. You don't know—"

"Enough!" Peyton slammed her hands down on the table. Her sudden burst of anger had the desired effect, and Sandra fell silent. She shrank back as Peyton rose, towering over her. "I found where Lilia was living when she gave birth to Grace. She left there Thursday morning to see family, but Lilia didn't call me until late Thursday afternoon." She glowered down at her aunt. Pity filled her, but she didn't give in to it. Sandra was the kind of person who only responded to strength and threats.

She was also someone who had chosen a man over her daughter. Many times. Peyton was counting on her to do it again.

"I know she came to see you, Aunt Sandra, so cut the theatrics and start talking. Otherwise, your boyfriend is going to prison for the next ten years."

Sandra's chin trembled, and she nervously licked her lips. "Okay. Okay. Yes, I saw Lilia."

Peyton reclaimed her seat. Now they were getting somewhere. "What happened?"

"She came by the house." With a shaking hand, Sandra took a shot from her water bottle and then grimaced. "Lilia had the baby with her, and she didn't want to come inside, so we talked in her car where it was warm. She said that Cade was looking for her. She'd run off before the kid was born, and he was mad about it."

"Was he abusing her?" Peyton already knew the answer to this question, but she wanted to figure out how much Sandra had lied about during their first interview.

Her aunt shrugged. "He smacked her around a few times. Who cares? All guys get irritated. Lilia made things worse by taking off with his kid."

"But you said Cade isn't the kind to care about a baby."

"That's what I figured, but I learned later he didn't like that Lilia took something that belonged to him."

Peyton could believe that. It was almost exactly the same thing Cade said to her. "Why did Lilia get involved with Cade in the first place? Didn't she realize he was a criminal?"

"Not in the beginning. Cade had money, and he showered her with gifts and made her promises. She thought they were gonna get married and live a white-picket-fence life." Sandra snorted, wiping her nose with the sleeve of her sweatshirt. "Stupid girl didn't realize just how dangerous Cade was until it was too late. I tried to warn her, but she didn't want to listen to her momma. She was in love."

Peyton's throat tightened. Lilia had always led with her heart. It was the best and worst thing about her. That desperate need to be loved, to belong to someone, no matter the cost. Her self-destructive behavior came from the same place Peyton's had. From a sense of unworthiness.

And Peyton feared those bad decisions may have cost Lilia her life.

"What do you mean she didn't realize how dangerous Cade was until it was too late?"

Sandra's gaze dropped to the table as if she'd suddenly realized she'd said too much. Peyton pounded the table with her fist, making the sodas and the water bottle jump. "Do you want me to help Bobby or not?" She glared. "What did Lilia discover about Cade?"

Sandra swallowed hard. "He's a killer, okay? Lilia told me that Cade suspected his accountant was stealing from him, so he asked her to look at the books because she understands numbers. Well, Lilia figured out the guy was skimming money from every transaction. She told Cade, thinking he was just gonna fire the guy, but then she was watching the news and saw the accountant was murdered."

"Walter Jennings." Peyton's mind raced. She remembered coming across the accountant's murder while looking into cases connected to the Iron Serpents. The man had been shot execution-style, his body dumped on the side of the road. Cold-blooded murder. "What happened when Lilia found out he'd been killed?"

"She freaked. Cade denied it, but Lilia didn't believe

him. That's when she decided to leave for good. She made some kind of escape plan and fled. I didn't hear from her for a long time." She took a drag on her cigarette. "Then, out of the blue, she showed up with the baby. She told me that before leaving Cade, she'd stolen evidence of his crimes along with some of his money. She was gonna turn him in to the police. I tried to talk her out of it. I knew Cade would kill her if he found out, but she insisted it was gonna be okay."

Sandra sneered. "She was passing through Knoxville on her way to see you, Princess Peyton. She was counting on you to help her out of the mess she'd made."

Oh, Lilia. She'd left Austin for the long drive to Dallas to meet with Peyton but stopped in Knoxville to see her mother on the way. Her cousin had always wanted a close relationship with her mom. It didn't matter that Sandra had shown a lack of maternal instinct over and over again. Or even basic decency.

Peyton's jaw tightened as an unexpected punch of grief and anger hit her. She was practically vibrating with it. Drawing a breath in through her nose, she took a moment to pray for strength, wisdom, and patience. "What went wrong, Aunt Sandra?"

Sandra poured more alcohol from her water bottle into the plastic cup and then dumped in some soda. "What do you mean?"

"Lilia called me in a panic. She was terrified."

Sandra's hand stilled on her cup. For the first time since they'd sat down, something cracked behind her eyes. Not guilt exactly. Sandra wasn't built for guilt. But something close. Fear, maybe. Or the dim awareness that her choices had consequences beyond herself.

"Bobby came home, didn't he?" Peyton's voice was hollow. She could see it clearly, as if she'd been there. "Was he alone?"

Sandra drained her glass, her hands shaking so badly she had to hold the cup with both hands. Peyton reached over and ripped it from her grasp. The plastic cup flew across the room and slammed into the wall. "Was he alone?" she demanded.

"No." Unexpected tears welled in her eyes. "Marvis was with him. Lilia took one look at them and went white as a sheet. She threw me out of the car and took off. They followed her."

Peyton had no doubt they did. Lilia had been terrified. For herself. For Grace.

And for Peyton.

She'd told Sandra her plan. To go to Peyton for help. But once the Iron Serpents were on her tail, she hadn't wanted to lead them straight to Peyton, so she called instead and set up the meeting at the train depot.

All this time... Her aunt knew everything, and she'd hidden it. Peyton gritted her teeth, her hands balling into fists. "Why didn't you tell me any of this days ago?"

"Because Bobby would've killed me if I had! He warned me not to say a word." Tears spilled over Sandra's cheeks. "I told you what I could! And I paid for it!" She waved her injured wrist before sagging against the chair, broken and deflated. "This isn't my fault."

"Where did she go?" Peyton didn't recognize her own

voice. It was cold and hard. "If she needed to hide, where would she go?"

"I don't know."

"Where, Aunt Sandra?" Her voice rose again as she towered over her aunt. "For the love of God, if you have ever had one ounce of motherly instinct, now is the time to find it. Where would Lilia go if she was scared and needed to hide?"

Sandra shook her head, dissolving into sobs. "I don't know." She placed her hands over her face and started rocking. "This isn't my fault. This isn't my fault."

The words rang hollow. Sandra could've done right by her daughter, but she'd chosen her boyfriend and her addiction over Lilia. Again. It was a vicious cycle.

And suddenly Peyton was weary. She wanted to lie down and weep. Because she believed her aunt was telling the truth. When Lilia ran away from Cade the first time, she went to a women's shelter in Austin. The second time... she'd called Peyton.

Within half a heartbeat, her aunt shifted from sadness to rage. She ripped her hands away from her face and practically fell out of the chair to fetch the plastic cup. "You should've protected her, Princess Peyton! This is all your fault."

The door to the interrogation room opened, and Dawson entered. As Sandra poured herself another drink and continued to fling accusations and insults, he wrapped an arm around Peyton's waist and led her from the room. The noise of the bullpen was barely audible. It was as if she'd stuffed cotton in her ears. Dawson steered her into a conference room and shut the door. Then his arms came around her. Strong, solid, dependable.

Peyton clung to him. "Marvis saw her." The realization sank in like sharp claws. "Cade doesn't have her. We suspected it. He told us so. But now we know for sure. It's Marvis. He has her."

"Every law enforcement officer in the state is looking for Marvis. We'll find him."

But would it be in time to save her cousin's life?

Or were they already too late?

TWENTY-ONE

Darkness pressed around Dawson as he slipped around the edge of the barn on a perimeter check. The scent of freshly cut grass mixed with the promise of rain. Clouds hid the moonlight, but it didn't matter. He could've navigated it in his sleep.

A twig snapped. Dawson whirled toward the sound, his fingers flying to his weapon.

Walker Montgomery stepped out of the shadows. Dressed in black tactical pants and jacket, the former Navy SEAL blended in with the night. An AR-15 was slung across his chest. "Don't shoot me, Detective."

"Might want to announce yourself."

A grin lifted the corners of his mouth. "Why do you think I stepped on the twig?"

Dawson chuckled, letting his posture relax. He hadn't needed to do the perimeter check, not with members of the Special Forces acting as bodyguards. But the interview with Sandra had left him edgy and restless.

Plus he had to check on the horses. His mom and dad were visiting his sister, her husband, and the twins a few hours away. They'd probably spend the night. Thunderstorms were moving in, and his dad's eyesight wasn't as good as it used to be.

"Any sign of trouble?" Dawson asked.

"No. Nathan's covering the north side of the property. We check in regularly, and he'll alert me if there's an issue." Walker checked his watch. "We change shifts at 2300. Jason and Logan will take over."

"I appreciate everything y'all are doing. My mom left some casseroles in the fridge, and there's always coffee, water, and soft drinks in the kitchen. Snacks in the pantry. Help yourselves." Dawson smiled. "Hayley told me she sends snacks with you, but she warned that, and I quote, you raid the fridge like a wild raccoon."

Walker's grin widened. "That woman dares to call me a wild raccoon. She's five months pregnant and eating everything in sight." He shook his head with the unmistakable pride of a man completely besotted with his wife. "We ordered Thai the other night, and she ate all the egg rolls. Crumbs were the only thing left in the bag."

Dawson shot him a warning look. "I'd be careful about mentioning how much your pregnant wife eats. Especially if you plan on having more children."

"Right you are. I stand corrected."

They both laughed. Hayley was known for her good sense of humor and wouldn't have found anything her husband just said as offensive. In fact, if she'd been there, she would've dished it right back to him.

With a final wave, Dawson headed back toward the house. The conversation and the warm way Walker spoke about his wife struck a chord. He'd had that once. With Peyton. He missed it. The inside jokes and shared meals. Someone to laugh with after a long day. He could've tried to build that with someone else after the divorce but hadn't wanted to.

He wanted Peyton. No one else would ever do.

Dawson entered the quiet house. It was late, after ten. A faint murmur from the living room drew his attention. He slipped off his jacket and shoes and quietly drifted into the living room. Peyton sat in a rocking chair, the warm glow of a side table lamp caressing her features. Nestled in her arms was Grace. The baby sucked a bottle with vigor, eyes fixed on Peyton's face while she sang a soft lullaby.

The peaceful scene was tender and sweet. Dawson couldn't help but think of Samuel. Grief rippled through him, but the pain wasn't as sharp or as harsh as before. Instead, it melted into something warmer. Gentler. A bittersweet ache that held both the loss of what they'd never have and the unexpected gift of what was right in front of him. Peyton, singing to a baby she hadn't expected to love. Grace, trusting her completely.

Samuel would never be in her arms. That truth would always hurt. But watching Peyton with Grace, Dawson realized that the love he'd stored up for his son—all that fierce, boundless, ready-to-burst love—hadn't disappeared. It'd just been waiting.

Peyton must've registered his presence because she

glanced up. Their gazes met. Her expression, softened by talking to the baby, shifted to understanding. A beat passed between them, one that needed no words. Then her lips curved into a smile. "Hey."

"Hey." He stepped into the room, drawn in by her silent invitation. "From tangling with bikers to feeding a baby. You're like a Swiss Army knife."

A soft laugh escaped her. "It's been an interesting week, that's for sure." Peyton tilted her head to look down at Grace again, and tenderness swept over her face. "She's so beautiful."

"She is. And a good eater. An expert crier. So-so in the sleep department."

"Not anymore. Your mom's sling trick has made her an expert sleeper." Peyton wriggled the bottle free from Grace and then positioned the baby on her shoulder to burp her. She winced with the movement, probably from the pull on her wound.

Dawson crossed the room and held out his hands. "Give her to me before you rip a stitch open."

Peyton scowled. "You're as bad as your mom. You'll think of any excuse to grab her away from me."

He kissed her lightly as he took the baby. The move was automatic. As natural as breathing. And when he tucked Grace on his shoulder and began patting her back, warmth and tenderness spread through him. She smelled of baby powder and soap and a touch of milk.

Peyton rose from the rocking chair and carefully lifted Grace's head to place a burp cloth on Dawson's shoulder. Then her expression shifted, the lightness leaving her eyes. Dawson paused in patting Grace on the back to brush a strand of Peyton's hair back from her cheek. "I know you're worried."

"I've been praying." She sighed. "For Lilia, of course. But also asking for forgiveness. I lost my temper with my aunt today. Nana Grace always preached patience and understanding, and grace. She'd be disappointed in me."

"I wouldn't be so sure about that." Dawson returned to patting Grace's back. "There's such a thing as right-eous anger, babe. Jesus flipped over tables, don't forget. Sandra's addiction is awful, but she made choices. Deci-sions that hurt her daughter and slowed our investigation. You did what was necessary to get the truth out of her, and I doubt Nana Grace—or God—would fault you for it."

Grace let out a tiny burp, and Peyton smiled, but it didn't quite reach her eyes. She lightly touched the baby's back, her fingers brushing against Dawson's.

"I wish I knew where Lilia was. It doesn't make sense, Dawson. She would contact me if she could. It's getting harder and harder to believe that she's simply hiding out somewhere." Her expression was haunted. "Someone attacked Lilia at that train depot. We have the blood to prove it. Marvis could've grabbed Lilia and then sent men back for Grace and the backpack, probably assuming the evidence was inside. But I got in the way. All the other attacks—the kidnapping attempt, shooting at me and you—were Marvis, trying to either frame Cade or get his hands on the evidence. It's the only thing that makes sense, right?"

Dawson couldn't refute her. He'd considered the same scenario.

"I know the odds." Her voice grew soft as her chin trembled. "Lilia probably died on the night of the train depot attack, and we just haven't found her body yet. But I don't want to believe she's gone. Does that make me foolish?"

"No." He pulled her closer, into a sideways hug. "It means you have faith, even when things look bleak."

She snuggled into his embrace, and holding her, along with Grace, undid the last of his resistance. The shields he'd built. The fear. The stubborn refusal to risk his heart again. All of it crumbled, quietly and completely, in the space of a single breath.

He didn't want to say goodbye or let Peyton go. He never had. What he wanted was right here—messy and uncertain and terrifying—and he was done pretending otherwise. He pressed a kiss to the top of her head before releasing her in order to gently set Grace down in the baby swing. She fussed slightly before he turned on the device and it swayed. Her eyelids fluttered closed.

Drawing a breath, Dawson turned to face Peyton. His wife. His ex. His everything. "I love you, Peyton."

She froze, the baby blanket she'd been folding swinging comically from her hands. Her eyes widened and then filmed with new tears. "I love you too."

Undone by her emotions, he crossed to her. Gently, he removed the baby blanket from her hands and took them in his. "Things are a mess right now. I know. The timing is terrible. But I have a bad habit of hiding my feelings, waiting for the perfect time to share them with you, and it only created bigger problems." He squeezed her hands. "So I'm saying it. Out loud. I love you. I've never stopped. And I don't know what comes next, or how we rebuild something we both broke, but I know I want to try. If you do."

Tears spilled over her cheeks. She didn't bother to wipe them away. "I don't know what comes next either, but I know I want to face it with you by my side." Peyton drew in a breath to steady herself. "I hurt you, Dawson. Made promises and broke them. So I won't make any now. What I will say is that I'm not the same person I was five years ago, and if you give me the chance, I'll show you that. Every day."

"You already are. I see it, Peyton." He released her hands to wipe her tears with his thumbs. "We both made mistakes. But I believe in second chances."

"So do I."

She rose on her tiptoes, her lips brushing against his. Dawson pulled her closer, mindful of the injury at her side, and returned the kiss. His world centered, a peace settled over him unlike any he'd ever felt. This was right. He felt it. In his heart and soul.

God had been leading them here. Through the grief, the distance, and the broken years. All of it—every painful step—had brought them to this moment. And while the future wasn't certain, Dawson would never regret loving Peyton.

Grace fussed from the swing. Dawson broke off the kiss, his heart racing and his breath shallow. He glanced over his shoulder at the baby in time to see her lift her legs. An eruption echoed in the room. His eyes widened, and a laugh bubbled up. "Well, that's one way to ruin a romantic moment."

Peyton giggled and then held her side. "Oh, don't make me laugh. It hurts."

Dawson reluctantly released her to stand over the swing. "Think she's done?"

Grace sent up a wail of discontent as if to answer his question. Her little fists waved in anger. Dawson quickly unstrapped her from the swing. "Well, don't yell at me. You're the one who did it."

Peyton doubled over, alternating between laughing and wincing. "Stop, I beg of you."

He lifted the baby out of the swing, and his mouth dropped open. "Good grief, she's covered in it. Changing table, stat. This is gonna be a two-man job. We might have to hose her down." He winked. "I did that once with Oliver. Mom yelled at me."

Peyton gasped. "You did not."

"He was eighteen months old, and it was in the dead of summer." Dawson hurried to the guest bedroom, where his mom had set up a crib and changing table for Grace. "Oliver loved it. So did Marcus. I'm pretty sure he changed his poopy diapers like that all August."

He set Grace down on the plastic surface, but then Peyton pushed him out of the way. "I'll do it. I don't want you to get the hose."

"Want gloves? A gas mask?"

She pressed her lips together. "I'm going to bust a

stitch if you keep making me laugh, and then you're going to explain to the doctor what happened."

"I don't care," he teased. "I know all the doctors in Knoxville."

Peyton popped open Grace's onesie. The GPS tracker attached to the pacifier clip fell to the side, hitting the plastic mat with a thump. Grace flailed her arms and legs, dressed only in a lightweight T-shirt, and hollered. Peyton spoke to her in soothing tones, calming her, and then grimaced. "Okay, the hose might not be a bad idea. I'm pretty sure she's gonna need a bath." She reached for the wipes, pulling two out, and the empty package fluttered to the carpet. "Do you mind getting the extra wipes? They're in the backpack."

Dawson turned away, spotting the black bag in the corner. He unzipped the main compartment and rummaged through the remaining supplies. No wipes. He checked the side pockets. Empty. "I don't think there are any more."

"There has to be. Check the bottom."

He upended the bag, dumping everything onto the bed. A pacifier, two diapers, a rattle. No wipes. He was about to tell Peyton they'd have to improvise when the bedside lamp caught the front of the backpack at an angle. A few strands of thread along the edge of the logo patch shimmered differently from the rest. Newer. Tighter. As if someone had carefully cut one section of the patch and stitched it back into place.

Heart pounding, he ran his thumb across the seam. The fabric beneath the patch was stiffer than it should have been. Something was sandwiched between the layers.

"Never mind!" Peyton sounded breathless. "I found the extra wipes in the drawer..." She appeared by his side with a half-dressed baby. "What is it?"

"This patch. It's been mended." He fished out his pocketknife and carefully cut the newer thread. The patch lifted away, revealing a small slit in the nylon. He reached inside with two fingers and pulled out a USB flash drive, barely bigger than his thumb.

Peyton gasped. "Dawson..." Her face went pale.

"We had it the whole time." He stared at the drive, not sure he quite believed it was real. They'd searched the backpack over and over again, but the repair was so well done it was practically invisible. The faint reflection on the newer thread was their only clue, and even that wouldn't have been obvious under normal lighting.

Peyton recovered first, waving toward her laptop, which was resting on the bed. "Don't just sit there. Plug it in. Let's see what everyone is trying to kill us for."

TWENTY-TWO

Peyton rubbed lotion on a newly bathed Grace, who smiled and waved her hands. It was such a strange feeling. They'd made a giant break in the case, but her focus was centered on making sure Grace was clean, dry, and comfortable before anything else. A year ago, she would've been hunched over that laptop, sleep and food forgotten, working until her eyes blurred. But Grace had rearranged her priorities in a way Peyton hadn't expected. The evidence wasn't going anywhere. This little girl needed her now.

Dawson growled in frustration from his perch on the bed. "None of the birthday combinations worked, and we're wasting time. The sooner we access whatever is on this drive, the better. Penelope, our cybersecurity specialist, has programs that can run combinations to crack the password." He reached for his phone. "I'm calling the chief."

Peyton dressed Grace quickly, reattaching the pacifier clip with the GPS tracker to her undershirt before snapping the onesie over it. She listened to Dawson's half of the conversation.

Then he hung up. "Chief Garcia is going to bring Penelope and her equipment here. He's worried that Marvis and/or Cade is watching roads, and if they see us driving to the police station at this hour, they'll assume we uncovered something."

"Won't they think that if they see the chief arriving at the ranch?"

"He's going to coordinate with the Special Forces and sneak onto the property. But it'll take some time. Penelope is at home, and the chief wants to make sure they aren't followed." Dawson tapped on the trackpad to eject the drive. "Until we can access what's on this drive and make a duplicate, this is the only copy we have."

Grace fussed. She was sleepy after her bath. Peyton reached for the cloth sling hung on the closet door. "Hold Grace for me while I put this on."

"What about your stitches?"

"I'll be fine. She's not heavy yet. It's no different from carrying her." Peyton handed the baby over and then wound the fabric across her chest and around her waist, tying it securely the way Ellen had shown her. It pulled slightly at her wound, but the pressure was manageable. "Okay, give her here."

Dawson gently settled Grace into the wrap. The baby fussed for a moment, then nestled against Peyton's chest and sighed. Within seconds, her eyes were drifting shut. Peyton smiled. "Works every time." She laid a hand on Dawson's chest, feeling the steady beat of his heart. "Pray with me?"

He covered her hand with his own and bowed his head. "Lord, we thank You for leading us to this discovery. Help guide our next steps so that we can use this evidence to bring justice. Watch over Lilia. Keep her in Your hands, help her hold on to hope. And watch over us, Lord. Because we need You now more than ever."

"Amen." Peyton felt a peace envelop her. There was so much that was still uncertain. Was Lilia alive? Could they crack the code on this drive? Would she and Dawson be able to truly move on from their mistakes? Danger lurked beyond the safety of the ranch. But Peyton knew she wasn't alone. She had God. And Dawson. And other people—like Ellen and Raymond— who loved and cared about her.

She leaned into that. She had to. It was the only way to walk through the uncertainty and the fear.

Dawson leaned down and kissed her. Nothing but a brush of his lips against hers, but it was when he pulled back, and she saw the love shining in his eyes that her heart tumbled over itself. "I love you."

"I love you too."

His cell phone rang, interrupting their sweet moment. Dawson glanced down at the screen and stiffened before swiping the screen, putting the call on speaker. "Walker, what's wrong?"

"We've got an Iron Serpent headed for the house. Alone."

Peyton's hand instinctively went around Grace, as if

she could shield the baby with only that. Her chest tightened. "What does he look like?"

"Can't tell. He's wearing a helmet. But the bike is a Harley-Davidson Road King. Black with red pin-striping on the fuel tank."

Dawson frowned. "That's not Cade. He rides a blacked-out Street Glide."

"I'm moving to intercept. Keep Peyton and the baby inside." Walker hung up.

Simultaneously, they reacted. Peyton grabbed her holster and handgun from the nightstand as Dawson grabbed a bag they'd packed with baby supplies in case they needed to make a run for it. Then he caught her hand, hustling her down the hall to his parents' bedroom. It'd been strategically chosen due to its proximity to the woods flanking the east side of the house, and the multiple exits. They could escape through the patio doors, the bathroom window, or the mudroom off the kitchen.

Once the door was shut behind them, Dawson grabbed the laptop on the small desk in the corner of the room. He pulled up the ranch's security camera feed. Four grainy images split the screen—the front gate, the driveway, the barn, and the back porch. Peyton leaned over his shoulder, one hand cradling Grace against her chest.

On the driveway camera, a single headlight cut through the darkness. The motorcycle rolled to a stop near the front porch. The rider killed the engine and dismounted, pulling off his helmet.

Peyton's breath caught. Even in the grainy footage, the bald head and spider tattoo on his neck were unmistakable. "That's Ricky."

Walker materialized from the shadows, weapon raised. The audio was tinny through the laptop speakers, but clear enough to follow. "Hands where I can see them."

Ricky immediately did as he was ordered. "My name is Special Agent Richard Mercer. I'm working undercover for the ATF. I need to speak with Detective Dawson Graham and Special Agent Peyton Hughes immediately."

Dawson hit a button on the laptop. "Walker, bring him in."

Peyton's chest tightened. This was serious. By coming here, Ricky had blown his cover. He wouldn't have done that unless something big was going down. Her steps were hurried as she followed Dawson back down the hall, past the kitchen and into the foyer. Her stitches ached with the hurried movements, the weight of the baby too much for them. The doctor had warned her against lifting anything. But what was she to do? Grace needed her.

Walker and Ricky were already inside. Relief creased Ricky's rough features the moment Peyton stepped into view with Grace. "We need to get out of here. Cade knows you have the evidence, and he's coming with his men. He doesn't care who he has to kill, as long as he prevents that evidence from leaving this house. He also wants his daughter."

Dawson held up a hand. "Hold on. How could Cade possibly know—"

"He put spyware on your phones during the attack in the alley." Ricky's words were clipped, and even though Dawson had asked the question, the ATF agent's eyes were locked on Peyton. "Cade knew there was a chance you would go back on the deal you made. He wanted insurance."

Peyton's heart thundered against her rib cage.

"I got here as fast as I could," Ricky continued, "but they aren't far behind. We need to leave now. Where's the evidence?"

"How many are coming?" Walker snapped, cell phone in hand. He'd been relaying messages to Nathan, who was near the ranch hands' cabins on the north side of the property.

"Most of the gang. At least twenty men."

Gunshots erupted as Nathan's voice spilled from the cell phone speaker.

"We're under attack."

TWENTY-THREE

Shouting and more gunshots erupted before the call cut out. Nobody moved in the silence that followed. Then Dawson reached for Peyton and Grace as the faint rumble of motorcycles reached his ears. His phone vibrated on his belt repeatedly with alerts as members of the Iron Serpents breached the security system.

"To the truck! Now!" Walker hustled them out of the foyer, through the kitchen, and into the mudroom. He threw open the back door. A vehicle was parked on the side of the house, out of view. Their primary escape plan. But the approaching motorcycles roared louder, and in the next second, Walker slammed the door shut. "Get down!"

Dawson dragged Peyton and Grace to the floor as an array of bullets slammed into the house. Windows shattered, spraying glass all over the floor. Ricky belly-crawled in their direction as Walker, using the window ledge for cover, shot back. Grace, startled awake by the burst of noise, began screaming. Her panicked cries ripped through Dawson, and all he wanted to do was comfort her, but there was no time for that.

"Bedroom," he ordered, practically shouting to be heard over the sound of gunfire.

Peyton was already moving in that direction, keeping as low as possible while hurrying through the kitchen. Dawson followed, with Ricky bringing up the rear. The noise from the motorcycles and the gunshots faded as they entered his parents' room. He hurried to the glass window and parted the curtains with a finger, peering out into the night. The attackers hadn't made it to this side of the house, but they needed to move fast. Walker wouldn't be able to hold them for long.

"We need to keep moving." Dawson snagged the lightweight backpack with Grace's supplies. Peyton had given the baby a pacifier, quieting her screams to muffled sucking. He waved them forward. "Ricky, cover us."

"What's the plan?"

"We're escaping on foot into the woods. From there, we'll head due east until we reach my neighbor's property." It was a plan of last resort. They'd come up with contingency after contingency, but no one could've expected the entire biker gang to attack the ranch. It was an act of sheer desperation on Cade's part.

"I have a car," Ricky said. "After the alley, I stashed one on the south side of the property in case things went sideways. It's about half a mile through the woods, parked on the access road past the fence line. Closer than your neighbors to the east."

Peyton shot him a suspicious look. "You planned for this?"

"I plan for everything." Ricky's jaw tightened. "It's how I've stayed alive undercover for years while infiltrating dangerous groups like the Iron Serpents."

Reasonable. Dawson had never worked undercover himself, but he had friends who had.

Walker burst into the room. "They're coming. I'll cover you."

Dawson needed no further urging. He opened the sliding glass doors. Cold, damp air hit him as he stepped outside. Lightning lit up the sky, followed by the slow rumble of thunder. He stepped to the side to let Walker position himself in a defensive posture.

Slipping his hand into his pocket, he pulled out the USB drive. He pressed it into Peyton's palm and whispered, "Take this." Everyone here would do whatever was necessary to protect her and Grace. Dawson wanted the evidence with them too. That way, if they got separated, or worse, the evidence wouldn't fall into Cade's hands.

Their eyes met for a moment in the darkness. He felt her stiffen slightly and knew she'd understood his reasoning. Her lips flattened into a thin line of disapproval, but she didn't argue. She merely tucked the USB drive into the pocket of her jeans before adjusting the hold on her weapon.

"Go." Walker waved them forward. "Now."

Grabbing Peyton's hand, Dawson stepped out into the yard. Keeping in a low crouch, watching the darkness for signs of movement, he bolted across the grass. Drizzle dampened his hair. He felt, rather than saw, Ricky coming up behind them.

Gunshots rang out. Dawson saw the flash of a muzzle around the side of the house, but the answering sound of Walker's weapon confirmed he was bringing up the rear. Shouts echoed through the night. More men were coming. A fresh dose of adrenaline coursed through his veins, and he put more urgency into his feet, pulling Peyton along with him. They burst past the treeline into the woods as a spray of bullets erupted. Bark from a nearby tree flew, pelting Dawson in the face. He barely felt the sting.

"This way." Ricky took the lead, driving them deeper into the woods.

The sky opened up. Dawson lost sight of Walker but could hear gunfire behind them. The Navy SEAL was doing his best to ward off the enemy for as long as possible, giving them the best opportunity for escape. Gratitude mixed with silent prayers as he begged God to protect Walker. To protect all of them.

Peyton used her jacket, which she'd grabbed after the attack started, to shield Grace from the downpour. It beat against the leaves and the trees, making it difficult to discern whether anyone was approaching. Dawson's shirt was soon soaked and stuck to his skin. He blinked water out of his eyes. Ricky was a few strides ahead. Peyton just in front of him. She was favoring her right side, and he could tell each step cost her.

Then she slipped. Dawson caught her before she and

Grace ended up on the ground. "You okay?" he whispered.

"Yes." She righted herself. "Are you sure we're doing the right thing by following Ricky?"

"He wants the same thing we do. To get the evidence into the right hands." Dawson scanned her face, her expression barely visible in the darkness. "What's the matter?"

"I don't know." She shook her head and adjusted the jacket over Grace. "It's nothing. Let's keep moving."

Dawson nodded, and they continued on the path. Ricky had slowed down, allowing them to catch up. He waved silently, as if to urge them on, and then pointed to a small path leading through the trees. Dawson knew it well. He'd used it many times to find his way back to the house. Ricky was taking them in the right direction.

Still, a niggle of doubt, caused by Peyton's suspicion, wormed its way through his confidence. Were they making a mistake to trust the ATF agent? They hadn't verified he was, in fact, law enforcement. They'd simply taken his word because they'd both deduced he was ATF before Ricky showed up on their doorstep.

Lightning burst across the sky, brightening the woods with a flash. Dawson caught sight of two bikers in the woods, closing in. He raised his weapon and fired. Ricky mirrored his movements. Screams from the men indicated they'd both taken a hit.

"Hurry!" Ricky ducked under a low-hanging branch.

Dawson urged Peyton forward. She broke into a run,

nearly slipping again on the slick path, before righting herself.

A shout.

Before Dawson could react, Peyton fired her weapon. A man hollered in pain. The woods were crawling with bikers.

God, help me get Peyton and Grace out of here!

They raced the last few feet to the road. Ricky was already in the car, the engine fired up. Peyton fumbled with the handle of the rear door before flinging it open. She dove into the back seat.

Movement out of the corner of his eye had Dawson whirling. He fired his weapon. A muzzle flashed, and a second later, pain ripped through his hip. He fell to the ground, inches from the open car door. Peyton's face appeared, little Grace's dark curls peeking out from the top of the sling. Dawson couldn't risk it.

"Ricky, get them out of here!"

Peyton screamed, "No!" as Dawson turned to fire again on the biker who'd just emerged from the treeline, his weapon pointed at the car. Gunshots rang out. The man fell to the ground.

Dawson collapsed against the muddy road, the rain pelting him, his leg throbbing with every beat of his heart, and watched as the vehicle holding the love of his life disappeared into the night.

TWENTY-FOUR

"We have to go back!" Peyton's pulse roared in her ears as Ricky spun off the dirt track onto a two-lane road. Grace let out a wail, and she wriggled the pacifier back between her lips. The baby immediately took it, her cries quieting. "Ricky, turn around. Dawson was shot. We can't leave him."

The rusty sedan plowed ahead at top speed. Ricky's jaw was tight, his hands locked on the steering wheel. Rain beat a relentless rhythm against the roof. Every second that put them farther away from Dawson made it harder to go back. Peyton thrust herself between the two front seats. She hardened her tone. "Turn around now."

Ricky's eyes flicked to the rearview mirror, but he said nothing. The car continued to accelerate. They were practically flying. Desperation took hold. Dawson had collapsed right before her eyes. There was no way of knowing how badly he was injured. He could bleed out right there, on that dirt road. She refused to let that happen.

"Stop this car. You know we can't leave him—"

Ricky slammed on the brakes. Peyton pitched forward between the seats, her injured side screaming as she threw her free arm around Grace to shield the baby. In that half-second of imbalance, Ricky's hand shot back and ripped the gun from her other hand. Then she and Grace were thrown back against the rear seat as he violently hit the gas.

Her gaze met his in the rearview mirror. Cold dread churned her stomach.

"I'd suggest you buckle up." His voice was flat. Unrecognizable. The desperate urgency from the ranch was gone, replaced by something hard and unyielding. "And stay quiet."

Oh God, no.

Peyton swallowed down the fear crawling up her throat and slid closer to the door. Trees whipped past. They were heading away from town, but Ricky couldn't maintain a high rate of speed forever. She needed to make a plan. To figure out how to get her and Grace away from him.

She touched the side panel of the door, searching for the handle. Her fingers found only smooth metal. Just a flat space where a handle should have been.

"You can't escape, Peyton, so don't try."

That cold dread moved like sludge through her veins. Goosebumps broke out on her skin. "You're working for Cade?"

Ricky was silent. His eyes stayed on the road, both hands on the wheel, as if she hadn't spoken at all.

"Marvis, then." She tried to keep her voice steady. Professional. As if she were conducting an interview and not sitting in a locked car with her baby and no weapon. "You're working with Marvis."

Nothing. Not even a flicker in the mirror.

The silence was worse than any threat he could have made. Threats she could negotiate with. Threats meant he wanted something and was willing to talk. Silence meant he'd already made every decision he needed to make, and none of them required her input.

Grace stirred against her chest, making soft sucking sounds on the pacifier. Peyton tightened her arms around the baby and forced herself to think. Panic wouldn't save them. Fear wouldn't either. Only her training and her God could do that.

Keeping her movements small, she searched the pockets of her jeans and then her jacket for anything to use as a weapon, but only came up with lint, a hair tie, and an old pack of gum. The USB drive Dawson had handed her was tucked in the coin pocket of her jeans. Did Ricky know she had it? Maybe. Maybe not. Either way, it wouldn't help her get out of this situation.

She was weaponless. Okay. Time to run through alternatives. Hand-to-hand combat would be impossible with Grace strapped to her chest. She could attack Ricky now, wrap an arm around his throat and use her body weight to choke him, but that would likely cause a car accident that would endanger Grace. Peyton had no issue risking her own life, but she wouldn't put the baby in a more dangerous position than they were already in. Whatever Ricky wanted, whoever he was working for, they wanted Grace alive.

Peyton, on the other hand, knew she wasn't likely to make it out of this.

Tears pricked her eyes. *God, if it's my time, then I accept that, but please... I beg you, save Grace. Do not let her fall into Cade's hands.* She wrapped her arms around Grace's tiny body. So small, so helpless. Peyton would do anything to protect her.

Her fingers brushed across the small GPS tracker attached to the baby's undershirt and tucked under her onesie. Her heart thumped twice as hope sprang free. If Dawson had survived the shooting, once he realized they'd been taken, he could use the tracker to find them.

It was a big if. Dawson could've lost consciousness or worse...

No! She shoved the thought aside. Faith meant having hope even when things were bleak. Peyton needed to be smart. Bide her time and wait for an opening to save Grace.

And she believed in her heart that Dawson would come for them.

The sedan slowed, and then Ricky made a sudden right turn onto a rutted road. They bounced down the short drive to a run-down farmhouse that looked like it hadn't been lived in for years. Paint peeled from the clapboard siding in long, curling strips. The porch sagged in the middle, and one of the front windows was covered with plywood. A single light burned behind a curtain on the ground floor.

Ricky killed the engine and got out, circling around to Peyton's side of the vehicle. He held his gun at the ready when he opened her door. "Turn around and put your hands behind your back."

Fear thrummed through her. "You don't need—"

"Do not argue, Peyton, or I will kill you here and now." His gaze was hard, his tone controlled and flat. "Do you want that? A gunshot at close proximity would damage Grace's hearing. Maybe permanently."

Dear heaven above, he meant it. He'd shoot her right here. Peyton stifled the shudder of horror that rippled through her and did as he ordered, turning her back to him and placing her hands behind her. The cold bite of metal wrapped around her wrists.

Handcuffs.

Ricky hauled Peyton out of the car, his rough grip sending a riot of pain through her side as her stitches pulled. Drizzle dampened her bare skin. Thunder rumbling in the distance promised more storms ahead.

He marched her up the sagging porch steps, the wood groaning under their weight. Grace whimpered at the jostling, and Peyton murmured softly to her, keeping her voice steady even as a fresh dose of terror ate her insides. Ricky shoved the front door open, the ancient hinges squealing in protest. Then he shoved Peyton across the threshold.

The inside of the farmhouse was barely better than the outside. Bare bulbs cast harsh light over peeling wallpaper and water-stained ceilings. The air smelled of mildew and stale cigarettes. A folding table sat in the center of what had once been a living room, a laptop open on its surface.

And there, in the corner, handcuffed to a radiator pipe, was Lilia.

Peyton's knees nearly buckled.

Her cousin was alive. Alive! But the relief was immediately doused as she registered the scene before her. Lilia's face was gaunt and hollow-eyed, her dark hair hanging in greasy tangles down to her shoulders. A bruise yellowed along her jawline, and her lower lip was split and scabbed. She wore a thin sweatshirt and jeans, both filthy, and her bare feet were tucked beneath her on the cold floor. She looked as if she hadn't eaten properly in days.

Then Lilia's eyes found Peyton. They widened. First with disbelief, then with something that shattered Peyton's heart. Hope.

"Peyton?" Her voice was a rasp, barely audible. Then her gaze dropped to the baby nestled against Peyton's chest, and a sob tore from her throat. "Grace? No... no, please—"

"Family reunion over." Ricky patted Peyton's pockets, unearthing the USB drive. Then he manhandled her over to a wall, forcing her to sit. His dark-eyed gaze bored into hers, sending a chill down her spine. "If you so much as breathe the wrong way, I'll kill you. Understand?"

The weight of Grace's small form strapped to her

chest in the sling set her priority. Bide her time. Search for an escape. Pray that Dawson was on his way.

She licked her lips. "I won't move."

He stared down at her, as if checking for any sign of deception. She forced herself to hold his gaze. Whatever he saw there must've satisfied him, because Ricky backed off, pulling a cell phone from his pocket. He dialed a number. "The package has been collected." He glanced down at the USB drive in his hand. "I've got everything. Get over here. It's time to finish this."

Peyton's attention shifted to Lilia. Her cousin seemed to be pleading with her eyes, but for the life of her, she couldn't understand what Lilia was trying to say. One thing she understood was that whoever Ricky was working with would be here soon. Once that happened, the opportunity to escape narrowed significantly.

Was it Marvis? It seemed the only thing that made sense. Ricky had somehow teamed up with the criminal. Was he even a real ATF agent? Peyton believed he was. Somehow, while working undercover, Ricky had betrayed his oath, trading his badge for something else.

Money, probably.

She flexed her wrists. The handcuffs were tight enough to bite into her skin. There would be no getting out of them. Peyton's gaze swept the farmhouse floor, searching for anything she could use as a weapon, but there was nothing but dust. Thunder rumbled, and the sound of rain battered against the roof of the old farmhouse.

Grace's eyes fluttered, and she wriggled as if waking

up, but then gave a few sucks on her pacifier and settled back down. They had maybe another half an hour before her next bottle. The backpack with the supplies had been with Dawson. They had nothing to feed her with, and Peyton was terrified of what Ricky would do if the baby started screaming. He'd been calculated and cold, but she sensed there was anger boiling beneath that calm exterior.

Ricky plugged the USB drive into the laptop. The desk was covered with old fast-food wrappers and loose-leaf papers. He pulled out the chair and sat down. "What's the password, Lilia?"

She remained silent. Ricky turned to face her, even as his weapon was pointed at Peyton. "I can and will shoot her from right here."

"You won't hurt Grace."

"I'll do what I have to do to get what I want."

His tone was deadly flat. Peyton's heart pounded against her rib cage as trembles raced through her. What kind of monster threatened to harm an innocent child? Lilia also looked stunned, as if she hadn't expected the threat against her baby. Then resignation washed over her face. She rattled off a series of numbers, letters, and symbols in rapid succession.

"Slow down," Ricky ordered. He typed the passcode in, but the file didn't open. "It's wrong. Start again, and this time go slowly."

Lilia did, but once again, the file didn't open.

Ricky growled in frustration.

"It'll be easier if you just let me type it." Lilia leaned

her head against the wall. Her complexion was pale, as if the very act of talking had drained her.

Suspicion crossed Risky's face. "If this is a trick—"

"It's not a trick." Lilia's voice was hollow with exhaustion. "You have Peyton and Grace. I wouldn't risk their lives. The password is thirty-two characters long. Numbers, letters, and symbols. I designed it so that no one could guess it or type it from memory. I have to see the keyboard."

Peyton kept her muscles relaxed, but her heart skipped a beat. Lilia was lying. Her cousin could count cards in a Vegas casino and do trigonometry in her head. A woman with that kind of mind didn't need to *see* a keyboard to type a password she'd created herself. She could have rattled it off perfectly the first time.

Which meant she'd given the wrong password on purpose. Twice.

What was she up to?

Ricky seemed to weigh his options. Then he crossed to Lilia and unlocked the handcuffs. "Try anything and I'll kill them both."

"I won't." Lilia rubbed her raw wrists and slowly—painfully—got to her feet. She swayed, grabbing the radiator pipe for balance. Peyton's heart ached watching her. Days of captivity had taken their toll. Their eyes met for the briefest of moments, and something in her cousin's expression hinted at a buried strength.

Then Lilia shuffled to the table and lowered herself into the chair. Her fingers hovered over the keyboard. Ricky stood behind her. Carefully, she pecked at the keyboard—another sign she was up to something since Lilia was an excellent typist—and then hit enter. The screen shifted as the USB drive opened.

A hunger appeared in Ricky's expression. His attention was locked on the laptop screen. "Where's the bank account number? The one that has all the money you stole from Cade."

Peyton shifted ever so slightly, using the wall to support her weight as she got her feet underneath her.

"It's buried in a folder." Lilia's fingers moved over the trackpad as her other hand disappeared from sight. "I'll pull it up for you."

"Quickly."

Lilia tapped on the trackpad, and something new filled the screen. Ricky's expression morphed into a slow smile as he leaned over farther. "Two million dollars. It's all here."

Without warning, Lilia's hand whipped out from underneath the balled-up food wrappers, a pen clutched tightly in her grip. She slammed it into Ricky's throat. He staggered back, howling, his hand flying to the wound. The gun clattered to the floor.

Peyton sprang from her position, lifting one leg and driving it straight into his chest before spinning around to swipe his feet out from underneath him. Ricky slammed to the ground. Movement out of the corner of Peyton's eye warned her to shift, and she stepped back just as Lilia, with every ounce of strength she had, slammed the folding chair against Ricky's head.

A sickening crack echoed through the room. He went limp.

Lilia panted, and the chair clattered from her hands. She looked ready to topple over. "Is he…"

"I don't know." Peyton wouldn't waste time trying to figure it out. Her duty was to save Lilia and Grace, and there were more criminals coming. "We need to get out of here. The keys to the cuffs. And the car. They're in his pocket."

Lilia dropped to her knees and rifled through Ricky's pockets, finding both sets. She stumbled as she struggled to her feet and nearly dropped the handcuff keys twice before she got one of the cuffs undone.

"Leave it." Peyton snatched the car keys from Lilia's other hand, the loose cuff swinging from her wrist. There was no time. "Grab the laptop. Don't leave it behind."

Lilia slammed the laptop shut, tucking it under her arm. Peyton scooped Ricky's gun from the floor, and they ran.

The front door banged open against the wall as they burst onto the sagging porch. Rain hit Peyton's face. Grace jolted awake and started wailing. The sedan sat where Ricky had parked it, ten feet away. Peyton hit the unlock button on the key fob, and the taillights flashed.

"Get in!" She yanked open the driver's door as Lilia threw herself into the passenger seat, the laptop clutched against her chest. Peyton slid behind the wheel, one hand shielding Grace in the sling, the dangling handcuff clanking against the steering column. She jammed the key into the ignition.

Headlights swept across the farmhouse as a van turned onto the rutted drive, blocking their only means of escape.

It was too late.

Peyton acted without thinking. She pulled a whimpering Grace from the sling and passed her to Lilia, saying, "Get down and stay down," pushing them both toward the wheel well. Thunder rolled, vibrating through Peyton, and she prayed the sound of the storm would muffle the baby's cries.

She eased open the driver's side door as the van rocked to a stop. Peyton immediately recognized it as the vehicle used in the attack against her and Dawson.

A man exited the driver's seat.

Marvis. Even through the rain, she recognized the lanky frame, and the unevenly cut hair plastered to his skull. He looked wilder than his mugshot—unshaven, strung out, his eyes darting between the sedan and the farmhouse. A pistol hung at his side.

All Peyton had was the element of surprise. He expected them to be in the house with Ricky.

She lowered herself behind the driver's side door, using it as cover. Rain pelted her head and shoulders as she pointed the gun at Marvis, taking aim. Doors slammed as two other men exited the truck. More members of the Iron Serpents. Peyton's heart thundered. Three to one. Not great.

Go to the house. Go to the house.

Marvis jerked his chin toward the front door, and the two men moved ahead, boots crunching on the gravel.

Peyton stopped breathing as they drew closer. Rain streamed down the window, distorting the glass. From his angle, the car should look empty. Lilia and Grace were curled in the passenger footwell, invisible in the dark.

The three men passed her heading for the house.

She let go of the breath she had been holding.

And then Grace set up a wail that carried over the sound of the storm.

Marvis's head snapped around. Peyton fired in rapid succession, sending the men scrambling for cover. Heart pounding, she collapsed into the driver's seat and fired up the engine. Lilia screamed as a gunshot ripped through the back window of the sedan, shattering the glass.

Peyton hit the gas. The car fishtailed in the mud as more gunshots rang out. She gritted her teeth as she clipped a tree attempting to make the turn onto the drive leading to the road. The steering wheel jerked in her hands, and the vehicle careened out of control, landing in a bush. The engine died.

"No!" Peyton frantically twisted the ignition.

Then the night exploded.

The woods erupted with movement. Voices—sharp and commanding—cut through the chaos.

"Police! Get on the ground! NOW!"

Peyton kept Ricky's gun raised, her body angled over Lilia and Grace. Tremors shook her body. It was impossible to tell who was who. Her finger hovered on the trigger, even as prayers lifted from her heart. Rain beat against the sedan, making it impossible to see. Icy air blew in through the shattered back window.

Then one large figure broke from the others. Limping. Favoring his left leg.

Dawson.

Relief crashed over her, so intense she nearly went dizzy with it. Peyton swallowed down the lump in her throat and ran her hand over Lilia's back. Her cousin was silently sobbing, clutching her child.

"We're safe, Lilia. We're all safe. You did it."

Lilia lifted her head, tears streaming down her dirty cheeks. "We did it."

Dawson wrenched open the car door. Peyton threw herself into his arms, holding on with everything she had, and knew, no matter what, she was never letting go.

"I've got you, babe," he whispered against her hair. "I've got you. It's over."

TWENTY-FIVE

Two weeks later

Dawson lay on the baby play mat next to Grace and jiggled a rattle in front of her. She was on her tummy, working hard to lift her head, her little neck straining with the effort. She managed a few wobbly seconds—enough to lock her dark eyes on the rattle—before her cheek dropped back to the mat. Then her face screwed up tight into the most heartbreaking expression, and she let out a wail.

"Don't cry, little one." Dawson gently rolled her over. Grace stared up at him, a tear leaking from one eye, and then a smile played on her lips. He grinned down at her, his heart warming at the way her eyes tracked his face.

"Dawson Graham!" Peyton appeared in the entrance of the living room, her hands on her hips. She looked stunning in a worn pair of jeans and a soft T-shirt that molded to her body in all the right places. Her hair was braided and fell over one shoulder. "Did you just flip that baby over? She's supposed to be doing tummy time."

"She doesn't like it." Dawson shook the rattle in front of Grace and was rewarded for the effort as the baby reached for the object.

Peyton's expression was exasperated but full of affection. "You're spoiling her."

"That's what uncles are good for." He grinned, not the least bit contrite.

She studied him with mock severity. "Uncle." Peyton lowered herself to the mat beside him, and his smile widened as he reached for her. The scent of her jasmine perfume tickled his nose. "That's presumptuous, don't you think? Who says I'm gonna agree to marry you?"

Dawson kissed her lightly and took pleasure in the way her hazel eyes darkened with desire and longing. "Something tells me I'll convince you."

She laughed, a blush creeping into her cheeks. Dawson didn't think it was possible, but he fell a bit more in love with her. Peyton had been staying on the ranch while they recovered from their injuries, and the last two weeks had only shown that the connection between them was stronger than ever. They'd gone on dates, talked for hours, and spent time with his family. They'd also started counseling together. Neither of them wanted to screw things up this time. Both were dedicated to building a strong foundation for their marriage.

Dawson was committed to giving their relationship

the time it deserved, he already knew, and had for a while, that he wanted to marry her again.

He tilted his head, a familiar ache in his chest, as his gaze drifted over Peyton's gorgeous face. "You look beautiful today, if I haven't mentioned it."

Her blush deepened. "You have. Three times at least."

"What's one more?" He cupped Peyton's cheek and rose up slightly to kiss her again, ignoring the way the move pulled on the stitches along his hip. The bullet had narrowly missed shattering the bone. He'd been very fortunate. They all had. It'd taken nearly a week to remove all the bullets fired during the biker attack ambush from the house and ranch property. But not one innocent person had been killed.

"Are you two smooching again?" Lilia's voice carried across the room.

Dawson broke off the kiss and glowered at her. "Yes. Do you mind?"

"Actually, I do. There's a juvenile in the room." She flounced in, her dark locks bouncing on her shoulders. Two weeks of Ellen's home-cooked meals had put a healthy color back into Lilia's cheeks. Physically, she'd be fine. Mentally and emotionally, things would take more time, but Lilia had also started counseling, and if her behavior was any sign, she was on the right track.

Lilia came to a stop next to the mat and smiled down at Grace. The love shining from her expression could've melted the hardest of hearts. "Sweet girl, why aren't you doing tummy time?"

"It's Dawson's fault," Peyton was quick to say.

"Hey! She was crying." He lightly pinched Peyton's thigh, causing her to squeal and shift away. "You're no better. You don't like it when she's upset either."

Peyton dissolved into laughter but tried to gather herself together long enough to mount an argument. "Not true! I can be tough when it's necessary."

"Both of you are liars." Lilia reached down and collected Grace from the mat, hugging her close. "If this keeps up, I'll have a wild child running around stuffed full of candy who doesn't listen."

Dawson shook his head, his lips twitching. "You can't use Marcus's kids as an example. They're like that because of their dad."

Lilia's mouth dropped open. "I wasn't…" She glared as she caught on that he was joking, but a laugh bubbled up in her throat. "Oooo, you are something else."

The doorbell rang before Dawson could make a smart remark. He used the couch for support in order to get to his feet, as Raymond answered the door. Voices carried from the foyer, and he immediately recognized Chief Garcia's low timbre. Concern vibrated through him, and he shared a glance with Peyton. They were having a cookout this afternoon, but guests weren't expected to arrive for another hour.

Ellen came out of the kitchen, wiping her hands on a dish towel. "Chief Garcia! Welcome." She offered him a brilliant smile, not at all ruffled by his early arrival. Dawson's mother adored guests, no matter the hour. "Can I offer you something to drink?"

"No, thank you, ma'am. Maybe in a bit." Chief Garcia removed his cowboy hat, his attention darting toward Peyton and Dawson. "Sorry to drop by early, but I had an update on the case and wanted to share it before the event this afternoon."

"Come in." Dawson waved a hand toward the couches. He suddenly felt edgy. "Have a seat."

Raymond and Ellen discreetly disappeared into the kitchen. Chief Garcia settled into the large armchair, while Peyton and Dawson took the couch. Lilia perched next to them, holding Grace close to her. She looked tense, and Peyton reached out to lightly touch her cousin's arm in a comforting gesture. Lilia took her hand and held it.

"Well, first, let me say that I appreciate y'all's patience while you let our department and the ATF piece together what happened." Chief Garcia settled his hat on the coffee table. "I'll start with Ricky. His real name is Richard Mercer. He was a legitimate ATF agent, embedded with the Iron Serpents for nearly three years. A series of events happened in quick succession."

He held up a finger as he ticked them off. "The murder of the accountant, Walter Jennings. Lilia stole evidence of the criminal operation along with two million dollars from Cade before disappearing. And the sudden arrival of Marvis Harrison, who claimed to be the legitimate and rightful leader of the Iron Serpents." Chief Garcia lowered his hand. "By this time, Ricky had become corrupted by the money flowing in and out of the biker gang. He'd also been pretending to be loyal to Cade for years as part of his undercover work, and knew Cade would never tolerate paying anyone a large sum of money, no matter what was at stake. So... he turned his attention to Marvis.

"Marvis was desperate to take down Cade. Desperate enough to make a secret agreement with Ricky. They would find Lilia and Grace. When they did, Ricky would get the two million dollars Lilia stole, and Marvis would use the evidence and Grace to blackmail Cade into stepping down."

Dawson's gut churned with disgust. He'd already guessed some of the story. "Let me guess, Ricky couldn't find Lilia."

"No. Not until Marvis and Bobby saw her at Sandra's house. Marvis called Ricky, who knew he had to act fast." The chief's expression softened with sympathy as his gaze went to Lilia and Grace. "Ricky figured you wouldn't drive to Peyton's, since you'd be worried about the Iron Serpents following you, and there are only so many places in Knoxville to hide."

"They ambushed me at the train depot," Lilia said softly, her voice haunted. "I was lucky to have hidden Grace before they found me. Ricky took off with me in my car but ordered the guys with him to grab Grace." She hugged her baby closer. "I was scared they'd find her."

Peyton bumped her shoulder against her cousin's. "But they didn't. Cuz I was there."

"Hey, you can't take all the credit," Dawson protested. He waved a hand. "Hello... I was there too."

Peyton grinned at him. "No one likes a braggart, Graham."

Everyone laughed.

Chief Garcia waited until the room settled and then continued. "What Marvis didn't know was that Ricky intended to double-cross him. Once he had the money and the evidence, his plan was to eliminate Marvis and Lilia, turn the evidence over to the ATF while secretly pocketing the money. He intended to walk away a hero. Decorated agent brings down a major criminal organization. No one would've questioned it."

Dawson could hardly believe his ears. Nothing was worse than someone who betrayed their oath to serve and protect. "Except he couldn't do that without the evidence."

"Correct. Every attack after that—the hotel, the highway, the sniper—was Marvis either trying to recover the evidence or an attempt to frame Cade, so we would keep the pressure on him. Ricky stayed in the shadows, letting Marvis take the risks while spying on Cade for him. He also kept feeding the ATF just enough intelligence to maintain his cover." The chief's expression hardened. "He purposefully provided false information and specifically said that our meddling in the Iron Serpents was enough to ruin the whole op."

Peyton shook her head. "That's why SSA Fallon was so upset in your office."

The chief nodded. "Yes, Ricky lied to his handler about Lilia's disappearance, so when SSA Fallon informed us that the Iron Serpents didn't have her, he thought he was telling us the truth."

"He was playing everyone."

"Yes, and it nearly worked. Thankfully, it didn't. After Ricky finishes recovering from his cracked skull, he'll be escorted to a nice cell to live out the rest of his days. Cade and Marvis too. Using the evidence Lilia stole, along with the arrests from the ranch ambush, we have enough to completely dismantle the Iron Serpents. All of them are going to prison." Chief Garcia gave them an appreciative look. "Y'all have been through a lot, but I hope knowing it brought down an entire criminal organization gives you some measure of peace."

Lilia looked ready to cry. "Thank you, sir."

"No, thank you. Your bravery and willingness to do the right thing put this in motion." Chief Garcia rose. "Now, if you don't mind, I believe I smell your momma's peach cobbler. I might steal a bit for myself before all the other guests arrive."

He left the room. Dawson shared a worried glance with Peyton. A single tear slipped down Lilia's cheek.

Peyton tilted her head to catch her cousin's gaze. "Lilia, hon, are you okay?"

"It's over." Her lips curved up into a smile, but it didn't reach her eyes. "I just... I'm relieved. Of course I am. We're all safe now, and that's wonderful. But..."

"But?"

Her shoulders sagged. "There's no more reason to stay here. On the ranch." She pressed her cheek against Grace's curls. "I know it sounds silly, but these last two weeks have been the happiest I can remember. Ellen teaching me to cook and helping me study for my GED. Raymond reading to Grace every night. All the kiddos running around, and people just popping by. Attending church all together." Her voice thickened. "I've never had this. A big family. People who actually want you around. It's like being wrapped in a warm blanket, and I'm not ready to give it up."

"Then don't." Dawson leaned forward, knowing this was the perfect time to share his secret. "I spoke to my mom and dad about it a few days ago. There's a set of empty cottages on the west side of the ranch. We rent them out sometimes in the summer to people looking to stay in Knoxville while visiting family, but otherwise they're empty. We'd like to offer one to you and Grace, Lilia. You are welcome to stay as long as you like."

Her mouth dropped open. "Really?"

"Really. Go ask my mom if you don't believe me."

Lilia sprang from the couch and took three steps across the room before turning back. She hurried to Dawson and enveloped him in a sisterly hug, mindful of the baby between them. "Thank you."

His throat tightened, making it hard to talk. "It's nothing."

Lilia practically skipped from the room, and the sound of excited voices spilled from the kitchen. Dawson smiled, envisioning his mom in tears. She'd been heartbroken at the idea of Grace and Lilia moving away. His entire family had grown quite attached to them.

Peyton stared at Dawson incredulously from her

place on the couch. Then she laughed lightly and shook her head. "I shouldn't be surprised, and yet, somehow, you always outdo yourself. Just when I think I can't love you more, you prove me wrong."

She leaned forward and captured his mouth with hers. Dawson took her face in his hands, losing himself in the world only they knew. It was sweet and passionate. Tender and reverent. He tasted forever on her lips. His heart thundered, and when they parted, he was breathless. "I have to admit, inviting Lilia to stay was selfish on my part."

Peyton nestled herself into the curve of his arm. "How so?"

"Well, for starters, I didn't want to listen to my mom complain and carry on about missing Grace. This way, she can babysit while Lilia is taking her GED classes. Win-win in my book."

"Right. Makes sense." Peyton chuckled against his chest.

"I was also hoping that having Lilia here on the ranch would tempt you into visiting more often." Dawson felt her still. He rubbed a hand down her back. "I know you have to go back to Dallas soon, but the cottage is yours whenever you want it. And the drive isn't so bad on weekends. I'll come see you too."

Peyton pulled back to look at him. That smile again, the one he knew well. It meant she was five steps ahead of him. "What if I told you I don't need a weekend cottage?"

His brow crinkled. "What do you mean?"

"I put in for a transfer to the Austin division, and it was accepted today. I was going to tell you about it after the party." Her smile widened as a touch of mischievousness glinted in her gorgeous hazel eyes. "That is... if you're okay with it? I mean, I could go back to Dallas and—"

"No!" He put a finger to her lips to stop her from finishing her sentence. "I am more than okay with it. The cottage is yours."

Her expression softened. "A second chance. For all of us."

"Yes." He trailed a finger across her chin and over her jaw, feeling like the luckiest man in the world. "I love you, Peyton."

"I love you too."

From the kitchen, laughter erupted—Ellen's bright and warm, Lilia's lighter, Garcia's deep rumble underneath. Grace fussed somewhere in the middle of it all. The sound of family. Messy, imperfect, and exactly right. Peyton kissed Dawson's cheek and then got up from the couch before extending her hand to him. "Come on. Let's get some peach cobbler for ourselves before everyone else eats it all."

He slipped his hand into hers and stood. "You don't have to tell me twice." The sound of car doors slamming outside caught his attention. His eyes widened when he spotted his brother. "Quick! Marcus and the minions are here. We have to hurry."

Peyton's laughter echoed through the house as he pulled her toward the kitchen, and it was, Dawson decided, the most beautiful sound in the world.

TWENTY-SIX

The Graham family had gone all out. Strings of lights crisscrossed the back porch and extended to the barn, casting a warm glow over the long tables laden with food and the clusters of people scattered across the yard. Country music drifted from a speaker someone had propped on the porch railing. Kids chased each other between the legs of adults, their shrieks punctuating the laughter and conversation. In the distance, the sun was slowly setting.

Detective Liam Miller wove through the party, saying his goodbyes. Dawson stopped him by the dessert table. "No, man, you can't go yet. We've got games planned, and we need smart people on our trivia team."

Peyton shifted Dawson's nephew, Oliver, on her hip and laughed. "At least three other people have told us they want you on their team, and Dawson lied and said you'd already agreed to be on ours."

"I did not lie." Dawson scowled. "I merely created

my team in my head and now I'm sharing it with everyone."

Liam chuckled. "Sorry, guys, I gotta bail. Next time. But thanks for the party. It was great. Y'all went all out."

"It's the least we could do." Dawson took the wriggly Oliver from Peyton and then wrapped an arm around her waist. She leaned into the touch. "It's not every day we can say we took down a criminal organization and put killers behind bars. The good guys won this time. We should celebrate that."

He agreed. Liam knew firsthand what it was like to be haunted by a case. To never get closure, never capture the killer.

That thought weighed heavily on his mind when he reached Chief Garcia. His boss was elbow-deep in barbecue ribs, looking more relaxed than Liam had seen him in weeks. He hated to ruin it, but there was something that needed to be addressed. "Sorry to disturb you, sir, but I'm heading out. Before I go, I wanted to discuss the email you sent me. About the true-crime podcaster who wants to do a feature on the Sarah Vance murder."

His boss wiped his hands on a napkin, tearing it up in the process. "It's unorthodox, but the mayor seems set on the matter."

A point that frustrated Liam to no end. Mayor Calhoun had already shared the news with the city council, and rumors were spreading through Knoxville. "That case remains ongoing and unsolved. It's a mistake to allow a civilian to run around town interviewing people about the murder." Liam's expression hardened. "I haven't given up on finding the killer."

"I know you haven't." Chief Garcia sighed. "Let's have a meeting about this on Monday. We'll discuss it then."

Liam would've preferred to settle the matter now, but he knew it wasn't Chief Garcia's call. The request for cooperation had come directly from the mayor's office. Declining it would require a concrete reason—something difficult to produce for a case that had gone stone cold years ago. But Liam was determined to try.

From his way of thinking, it was shameless to use the gruesome details of a young woman's murder to boost ratings and line pocketbooks, but he doubted the mayor would agree with him.

So he'd have to find another reason.

Resigning himself to a long weekend reviewing Sarah's case file, he drove away from the Grahams' house toward town. The route took him past the cemetery on Route 12. It always did, no matter which direction he was headed. He'd stopped noticing it most days. Tonight, with Sarah's name fresh on his tongue and the frustration of the podcast still simmering, his foot eased off the gas, and he turned in.

The cemetery was quiet in the fading light. He parked near the east gate and sat for a moment, hands on the steering wheel, before climbing out. He didn't have flowers. Hadn't planned on coming. But Sarah wouldn't mind. She'd never been the type to care about gestures.

At least, that's what the case file told him. He'd never actually known her. Not while she was alive, anyway.

The gate squealed on its hinges and then banged shut behind him. Liam traversed the pathway by muscle memory. It wasn't the first time he'd visited Sarah's grave. Probably wouldn't be the last. A giant oak blocked out the last remaining rays of sunlight, and a chill raced down his spine. His lightweight button-down, perfect for a sunny spring day, offered little protection against the rapidly falling temperatures.

The cemetery was silent. No mourners. No groundskeeper. This section was older and often forgotten. Some of the tombstones crumbled from age and time. Sarah's was near the back, tucked next to her maternal grandparents, who'd long since passed.

Hers was a modest stone. Gray granite. Nothing fancy. As far as Liam knew, no one visited this grave.

Except him.

He dusted off the dirt covering her name, tracing the carved letters with his fingers. "Hey, Sarah. It's been a while, huh?" Memories assaulted his senses. The flashlight beam sweeping across the grass, catching on one pale arm barely visible in the brush. Liam pushed the image away. "We're coming up on ten years. I don't know what to say about that, except that I haven't given up. I'm still fighting. You should know that."

A slight wind rustled the leaves of the oak tree and sent the overgrown grass tucked up close to Sarah's grave tilting to one side. A flash of white caught his eye. Something was nestled at the base of the headstone, half-hidden by the grass. Liam leaned closer.

A paper. Weighted down by a rock.

Liam stilled, just staring at it. Then he pushed the rock aside and picked up the paper with the edge of his fingers. It looked clean. Recently placed. Gingerly, using only the edges, he unfolded the sheet.

His breath stalled.

A hand-drawn sketch. Pencil on plain white paper. A small sunflower, delicate and detailed, each petal rendered with care. A replica of the one drawn on Sarah's hip by her killer. And underneath, scrawled in messy letters, were two words.

I'm sorry.

Texas Ranger Heroes Series

Ranger Protection

Ranger Redemption

Ranger Courage

Ranger Faith

Ranger Honor

Ranger Justice

Ranger Integrity

Ranger Loyalty

Ranger Bravery

Ranger Purpose

Triumph Over Adversity Series

Calculated Risk

Critical Error

Necessary Peril

Strategic Plan

Covert Mission

Tactical Force

Badge of Honor Series

Fractured Memories

Dangerous Lies

Broken Silence

Shattered Hope

Would you like to know when my next book is released? Or when my novels go on sale? It's easy. Subscribe to my newsletter at www.lynnshannon.com and all of the info will come straight to your inbox!

Reviews help readers find books. Please consider leaving a review at your favorite place of purchase or anywhere you discover new books. Thank you.